This book belongs to

_____

_____

D1469125

Best Loved
GOODNIGHT TALES

Best Loved
GOODNIGHT TALES

SIENA

THIS IS A SIENA BOOK

SIENA is an imprint of PARRAGON

Parragon
13 Whiteladies Road
Clifton
Bristol BS8 1PB

ISBN 0-75252-919-6

Printed in Great Britain

Designed by Mik Martin
Cover illustration by Terry Rogers

CONTENTS

IF HE HAD said it once, he had said it a hundred times. Poor Farmer Forrest was in despair. At any time of the day you might see him look up from his work towards the top meadow and cry in exasperation, "Now where's that sheep?"

Yes, Molly was a sheep who loved to wander. She wasn't a stay-at-home-and-wait-for-your-wool-to-grow kind of sheep at all. At the sight of a lowish wall, a thinnish hedge or a weakish fence, Molly was off. She didn't run or make a noise or draw attention to herself in any way. She simply trotted off down the lane. It was sometimes hours before anyone noticed she was gone at all.

But after her fourth escape attempt, Farmer Forrest became wise to Molly's ways. He put her in the top meadow, where he could keep an eye on her. Whenever he lifted his eyes from his work, he checked to see that she was there. But still the

cry was heard at least once a week.
"Now where's that sheep?"

To be fair, it wasn't really
Molly's fault. You see, Farmer Forrest
didn't keep sheep as a rule. He had
cows, pigs and a few hens, but he
had never farmed sheep. It was only
when Mrs Forrest took up spinning
that she begged her husband to
invest in a flock.

"But I don't know anything
about sheep!" complained her
husband. "Besides, this isn't the right
kind of country for them. No one for
miles around has sheep. Can't you
just buy a fleece to spin?"

But Mrs Forrest argued that it
just wouldn't be the same. To spin

wool from a sheep that had lived on your own land, that would be really satisfying.

"And I can just see you wearing the jumper I would knit," she told her husband. Think how proud you would be."

"All right," said Farmer Forrest, "but not a whole flock. We'll start with one sheep and see how we get on. That's only sensible."

Mrs Forrest reluctantly agreed, but in fact this was very far from sensible. You see, sheep are sociable animals. They like to be with a whole group of their own kind. They're not loners at heart. That was why Molly set off to find some like-minded sheep at every opportunity. As I said, it really wasn't her fault.

But Farmer Forrest found that he was wasting an enormous amount of time running around the countryside looking for that sheep. She nearly always trotted off in the same direction, as she had a strong feeling that there were other sheep to the north of her, but even so, there were many winding lanes around Forrest Farm, and it sometimes took the farmer the best part of a morning to find her.

"You know," Farmer Forrest said to his wife, "this can't go on. You'll have to find somewhere else to supply you with wool. I can't keep spending time running after that sheep. I'm far too busy at this time of year."

"Oh, but if you could just wait another couple of weeks, pleaded Mrs Forrest, "it would be time to shear her. Once I've got my fleece, you can sell her if you like, although I must confess that I've become rather fond of Molly. She's got such an independent spirit."

"Independent spirit my big toe!" scoffed her husband. As soon as she's shorn, that sheep can go and be independent somewhere else."

A couple of days before the shearing, as Mr and Mrs Forrest

were sitting at breakfast, Mrs Forrest raised the subject again.

"Honeybun," she began.

"Don't call me that," growled Mr Forrest.

"How would you like a whole flock of sheep like Molly?"

"We've been through this before," said Mr Forrest. "I've told you, I am not a sheep farmer."

"Well," said his wife, pointing with her cereal spoon, "I think you are now."

Mr Forrest followed her gaze. Up in the top meadow was a flock of sheep. Not one lonely Molly but at least fifteen sheep.

"What on earth…?" Mr Forrest

hurried from his chair and threw on his coat. This had to be sorted out.

But when he drew near the meadow, he found that his eyes had not been playing tricks on him. There really were fifteen sheep grazing happily on the juicy grass. And only one of them was Molly. To be honest, despite his many trips across the countryside to bring her

home, Mr Forrest wouldn't have been quite sure which sheep *was* Molly, but Mrs Forrest had followed him from the farmhouse, and she at once pointed out their own sheep.

"But where have these others come from?" asked Mr Forrest. "None of them have markings or collars or tags as far as I can see."

"I haven't the faintest idea," said his wife. "We'll have to think how we can find out who owns them. They do look *lovely* up here though, don't they?"

Mr Forrest grunted and went off to his work, while Mrs Forrest hurried back to the farmhouse.

The telephone was ringing as she arrived.

"Oh, Deidre," said a voice. "Thank goodness I've caught you. Something dreadful has happened. We've lost Hortense."

Mrs Forrest recognised the voice of one of the members of her spinning circle.

"Hortense?" she queried. "Is that your daughter?"

"No, no, no," cried the caller. "It's my sheep. The one I was going to have sheared next week. How am I going to find her?"

"Well, you could ask my husband," suggested Mrs Forrest. "He's had quite a lot of experience of finding sheep, especially just lately."

But even as she was speaking, Mrs Forrest was getting the funny feeling that she had seen Hortense rather more recently than her friend had.

"Let me call you back," said Mrs Forrest. "I just need to check something out."

Over the next few minutes, Mrs Forrest telephoned six of her spinning-circle friends. Every one of them reported a sheep that had gone missing during the past night. The farmer's wife felt pretty sure that other members would report a similar event.

"Oh, *clever* Molly," breathed Mrs Forrest. She realised now that the sheep must have made several friends in a similar situation as she roamed the countryside on her many bids for escape.

The sheep were so happy all together in the meadow that no one had the heart to send them all home — even Farmer Forrest. So Mrs Forrest became the official shepherdess of the spinning circle.

I wouldn't like to promise that Molly has wandered off for the last time, though. I did hear that there was a solitary sheep over in Farmbridge. And if I heard it, I expect Molly did too...

ONCE UPON A TIME, there was a group of boys who played in a band. They practised very hard and soon became so good that they were always invited to perform at the village fête in the summer and for the carol-singers in the winter. And very often, during the year, they would be asked to play a few tunes at a party, or a wedding, or a ceremony at the village hall.

Everyone was happy. The boys made lots of pocket money (which was just as well, because instruments are very expensive), and the village had its own little band it could call on.

There was only one problem,

and that was Eddy. Now Eddy played
the trumpet like an angel. *That*
wasn't the problem. He could sing
beautifully too, and sometimes did a
chorus of *Silent Night* when the
band trotted round the village with
the carol-singers. In almost every
way, Eddy was a perfect member of
the band, if only he wasn't always
late!

It didn't matter how carefully
the boys discussed their arrange-
ments beforehand, when they called
at Eddy's house on the edge of the
village, it was always the same.

"Are you ready, Eddy?" they
would shout.

"Nearly," Eddy would call back,

and the other boys would groan, because they knew what "nearly" meant. It didn't mean, "I've just got to put my socks on and I'll be with you." It didn't mean, "I'm running down the stairs right now." It didn't even mean, "Just let me comb my hair and clean my shoes and I'll be there." It meant, "Sometime in the next hour or so, I might be ready to join you."

As you can imagine, it drove the other boys absolutely wild. They had tried everything to solve the problem. Bobby had been appointed Eddy's "minder", responsible for making sure he was ready, but after two weeks, Bobby resigned. He couldn't bear the mess in Eddy's bedroom, and he couldn't bear the vague way in which Eddy did everything at home. When they were playing, it was quite different. Eddy always came in at the right places and had his wits about him. At home, he was a different boy.

"I know just how you feel, Bobby," said Eddy's mother, when she found Bobby sitting in despair at the bottom of the stairs, waiting for her son.

"I don't know what to do about him. He just doesn't seem to have any idea of time," she went on. "Getting him to school in the morning is a nightmare. We'll make

superhuman efforts to have his clothes and shoes ready. I'll stand over him until he's brushed his teeth and combed his hair. Then I'll just leave him to put his tie and shoes on. You wouldn't believe that a boy could take an hour to do something as simple as that."

"I would," groaned Bobby. "Oh, I would."

This state of affairs went on for so long that everyone had become used to it. The boys in the band took to calling for Eddy at least two hours before he was needed. By hanging around outside and shouting up to his window every ten minutes, "Are you ready, Eddy?" they would eventually manage to get him out of the house.

Eddy's mother grew used to getting up a couple of hours early to get her son off to school. It was ridiculous, but no one could see another way to do it.

Then Eddy's Uncle Albert came to stay. He wasn't a real uncle, in fact. He had gone to school with Eddy's father and had long been a friend of the family. Eddy had called him Uncle Albert since he was tiny.

Now Uncle Albert had not visited for several years, as he had been working abroad, so he did not know about Eddy's lateness. He was shocked the first morning of his visit to find his hostess downstairs at the crack of dawn. Eddy's mother explained the whole problem.

The next day was a Saturday, so

Uncle Albert looked forward to being able to sleep in without being disturbed, but once again he was woken horribly early. He came muttering out of his room to find Bobby waiting patiently on the stairs. There was a wedding at nine o'clock, and Bobby was making quite sure that Eddy wouldn't be late, as he was playing a solo.

Uncle Albert sat down on the stairs with Bobby and listened to the whole story.

"But this is ridiculous!" he said. "Haven't you tried to stop it? You can't let it go on."

So Bobby told Uncle Albert about all the efforts that had been made to improve Eddy's timekeeping. He explained that Eddy had been talked to, pleaded with, shouted at, encouraged and even rewarded, but that nothing had worked.

"I see," said Uncle Albert. "Have you tried doing nothing?"

"Well," said Bobby, "that's what we're doing now, really."

"No, no," said Uncle Albert. "I mean nothing as in *not* arriving early for him."

"But he'll be late," said Bobby.

"Yes," said Uncle Albert. "But at least then he'll realise the consequences of his actions. He's not a bad lad, but I don't think at the moment he has any idea how much trouble people go to for him."

"You're probably right," said Bobby. "But we can't start today. The wedding…"

"Yes, yes, I understand," said Uncle Albert. "But we will start on Monday. Agreed?"

Bobby told the band about the new plan, and Uncle Albert told Eddy's mother.

The boys in the band agreed that it was worth a try.

"After all," said Bobby, "nothing else has worked."

Eddy's mother looked doubtful, but she was at her wits' end.

"Frankly, Albert," she said. "I'm

willing to try anything. I'll leave it in your hands."

On Monday morning, no one shouted at Eddy to get ready for school. So he was late. By the time he finally wandered into the schoolyard, it was already time for morning break. His teacher told him not to let it happen again and gave him extra work.

On Monday evening, Eddy was so late for band practice that the other boys had gone home before he arrived. Eddy felt a little annoyed at this. They could have waited just a few minutes, couldn't they?

On Tuesday morning, Eddy was late for school again. This time the teacher was not so understanding. He gave Eddy extra homework and a lecture about punctuality.

On Tuesday evening, the band was supposed to be playing "Happy Birthday" to Mrs Marlow, who had celebrated her hundredth birthday that day. Luckily it was a tune that sounded all right without the trumpet, because Eddy failed to turn up at all.

On Wednesday morning, Eddy made an effort to get to school on time. It wasn't a very successful effort, because he was still twenty minutes late for his first class, but it was a start.

That evening, Eddy arrived at

band practice about five minutes before it ended. Things were slowly improving.

It took three weeks, and a really quite unpleasant session with the headmaster, before Eddy began to arrive at school on time. With no one to shout at him, being punctual for band practice took a little longer, but it happened in the end.

Now, it has become a tradition that the band stands in front of their trumpeter's house and calls, "Are you ready, Eddy?" But there is never any reply, for Eddy is down in the street shouting too!

The
Parrot
Problem

Miss Lavinia Blenkinsop was a very proper and particular lady. She ate her fruit with a knife and fork and always wore just the right amount of discreet jewellery. Her only regret was that the rest of her family was not so genteel. She tried not to let her friends meet them.

Then, one day, Miss Lavinia Blenkinsop had news that her Uncle Boris had died. She remembered how Uncle Boris had bounced her on his knee when she was a child. It was a shame, even though she hadn't seen the old rogue for years. Uncle Boris had been a sea captain in his youth and had sent his niece postcards from every part of the world. Rather unexpectedly, prim and proper Lavinia had had a soft spot for Uncle Boris.

A few days later, a van pulled up outside Lavinia Blenkinsop's immaculate gateway.

"Sign here, please," said the delivery man, carrying a large parcel with a big sign on it saying "This way up."

Miss Blenkinsop was very surprised, but she carried the parcel into the house and put it on the table. She saw that there was an envelope attached to it.

"Dear Miss Blenkinsop," said the letter inside, "under the terms of your uncle's last will and testament, this bird now belongs to you. It was your uncle's dearest possession, and he particularly requested that you should take good care of it."

Miss Blenkinsop smiled. A stuffed bird! How typical of Uncle Boris. Well, she needn't put it anywhere that anyone could *see* it. She undid the parcel, wondering if it would be a penguin from the North Pole or a flamingo from North Africa.

It wasn't. It was a parrot from South America — and it was alive!

Miss Lavinia Blenkinsop stared at the parrot, and the parrot stared at her.

"I'm a parrot!" he said, quite distinctly, in a loud voice.

Well, Miss Blenkinsop could see that. She had no idea how to look after a parrot, but she supposed that for Uncle Boris's sake she would have to learn. And after all, he would be a talking point. None of her prim and proper friends had parrots.

That afternoon, Miss Lavinia Blenkinsop had invited a select little party to tea. She placed the parrot in his cage prominently in the corner of the room and sat back to await reactions. She was not disappointed.

"My dear, how quaint!" said one lady in a large hat.

"What a novel idea! Isn't he a lot of trouble?" asked another.

"Not at all," said Miss Lavinia Blenkinsop. "He's as good as gold."

"Knickers!" said the parrot.

Yes, that's right. That's exactly what the parrot said, and just in case his shocked audience didn't understand him the first time, he said it again, even louder.

Miss Lavinia Blenkinsop turned pink, but she thought quickly.

"It's a Brasilian word," she said, "meaning 'Pleased to meet you.'"

The parrot made a rude noise.

"How clever he is," said his new owner. "That's a very polite term among the people of the Amazon."

Over the next few weeks, Miss B. tried to teach the parrot more polite terms, but you would be amazed how many Brasilian and Amazonian words he knew. And you would be amazed, too, if you could see how he made his owner laugh in private. It seems she had more in common with her Uncle Boris than she had realised.

So the parrot turned out not to be a problem after all. He has learnt lots of new words now — and so has Miss Lavinia Blenkinsop!

Granny Gumdrop

BELINDA climbed on to a chair and looked out of the window, as she did every day just after lunch. She held on tightly so that she didn't fall.

"Can you see her?" asked Ben.

"Yes, here she comes!" said Belinda with a giggle.

"Is she wearing her hat?"

"Yes!"

"Is she wearing her old coat?"

"Yes!"

"Has she got her boots on?"

"Yes!"

"And...?" Ben was giggling too.

"And she's got her umbrella. And it's open, it really is!"

"Silly Granny," said Ben.

The children took it in turns each day to look out of the window at the old lady. She wasn't really their granny, but they thought she looked so funny that they had nicknamed her Granny Gumdrop. They weren't usually unkind children. It was just funny the way she always dressed as if it was pouring with rain, even in the middle of the summer. Belinda and Ben had no idea that Granny Gumdrop could see them watching her as she went past.

But one day, when they were in the supermarket with their mum, the children were surprised to see a familiar figure coming round a stack of baked beans.

"It's Granny Gumdrop!" hissed Belinda, so loudly that the old lady couldn't fail to hear her.

"Why," said Granny Gumdrop, "if it isn't Hurly and Burly."

"Those aren't our names," said Ben, rather offended.

"No," said the old lady, "but Granny Gumdrop isn't *my* name. Why do you call me that, Hurly?"

Ben was younger than his sister and often alarmingly truthful.

"Because you wear a funny hat and funny clothes," he said.

"And do you want to know why I do that?" asked Granny.

"Yes," said Belinda and Ben.

"Well, why are you wearing a clown suit, Hurly? And why have you got that red hat on, Burly?" asked Granny Gumdrop.

"Because we like them," said

Belinda stoutly. "Why shouldn't we wear what we like?"

"That's exactly what *I* say," said Granny Gumdrop. "I *like* my hat, and my coat, and my boots. And I specially like my old umbrella. Why shouldn't I wear what I like?"

The children looked thoughtful, and Mummy smiled and invited their new friend to tea.

"That would be a pleasure too," said Granny Gumdrop.

THERE WAS ONCE a little girl called Sally who was not very truthful. Her mummy and daddy told her how important it was to tell the truth, but Sally didn't listen. She never told lies about things that really mattered, so she thought they were just making a fuss about nothing.

When I say that Sally didn't tell lies about things that really mattered, I mean that she wouldn't have dreamed of saying she was ill when she wasn't. And she would never have made something up about a friend or a stranger so that they appeared unkind or stupid. No, Sally's lies were about silly things. In fact, when she was a baby, her parents thought she simply had a vivid imagination, and they liked her little stories. But now that she was older, it didn't seem so funny any more.

Let me tell you the kind of thing that Sally would say.

"I've only got one sock on," she would announce at breakfast, "because I gave the other one to an elf this morning."

"Don't be silly, Sally," her mother would say. "Go and find your other sock and put it on."

"I can't eat my breakfast," the little girl would go on, "because a rabbit came in the night and borrowed my teeth!"

"Don't be silly, Sally," her father would say. "Eat up like a good girl."

Then it would be time for Sally to go to nursery.

"I don't want to wear my red coat," she would wail. "It's not a red day today. It's a blue day."

"Don't be silly, Sally!"

"There are creepy-crawly things in my boots! I can't put them on."

"Don't be silly, Sally!"

And so it went on. All day long, Sally made up stories about everything she did or saw.

If Sally saw some flowers growing by the path on her way to nursery, she would say, "I know the

fairy who planted those. Her name is Annabel."

Sally's mummy and daddy hoped that their daughter was just going through a phase that would soon pass.

"She's a very imaginative little girl," said Sally's teacher. "It would be a shame to bring her down to earth too much."

"Just a little bit would be nice," said Sally's mummy. "I never know whether to believe her or not when she says something out of the ordinary."

Of course, as time went on, everyone believed Sally less and less. They got so used to her stories and inventions that they hardly listened to what she said. So when Sally came running in from the garden one day with important news, her mummy didn't pay too much attention.

"There's buzzing in the garage," cried Sally.

"Don't be silly, Sally," said her mother, automatically.

Sally went outside to play for a while. But after half an hour, she came running back inside.

"They're buzzing in and out," she said. "Like this." And she did a little dance in the middle of the sitting room.

"Don't be silly, Sally," said her

mother. "No one is dancing in our garden."

"Not in the garden," said Sally. "In the garage."

"Don't be silly, Sally. The only things in the garage are the car and the bookshelves that your father started before you were born and still hasn't finished," said Mummy.

So Sally went out to look again. When she came back, she was

holding something tightly in her striped mittens.

"Look," she said. "I caught one of the buzzy things."

"Don't be silly, Sally. There's nothing in your hands at all."

"Yes, there is," retorted Sally, and she opened her arms wide.

Sally's mummy carried on with her work, but a second or two later she quite distinctly heard a buzzing sound. It was a bee.

Then Mummy shut the doors and windows and called Daddy down from his workroom.

"There's a swarm of bees in our garage," she said. "Sally discovered them."

Daddy looked doubtful for a moment, but Mummy and Sally spoke together.

"No," they said, "it's *true!*"

Some men came to take away the bees before they stung anyone.

Mummy and Daddy listen a little more carefully to what Sally says these days. Perhaps that's why Sally doesn't make things up quite so often — except when she doesn't want to wear blue socks, of course. Then those naughty elves *will* come and steal them!

The Busy Baker

ONCE UPON A TIME, there was a very busy baker. He was busy because his bread and cakes and biscuits were the most delicious for miles around. If a person tasted just one of them, he or she would never want to eat anything made by another baker again.

The baker made bread that smelled heavenly and tasted so good that some people ate it just by itself without cheese or jam or honey.

The baker made cakes that melted in your mouth and made you wish you could eat them for breakfast, lunch *and* supper.

The baker made biscuits that were the crispest and crumbliest you have ever tasted. Many an important person in the town walked around with telltale crumbs on his waistcoat!

But it wasn't only because his baking was popular that the baker was so busy. The fact was that he was never satisfied with the wonderful things he made. He always had to be trying something to improve them, or working hard to invent a recipe that had never been made before.

So the baker worked night and day. His chimney could be seen smoking at midnight, and he was up again to make bread for the morning by three o'clock.

Of course, it is much easier to work hard at something you like than it is to put a lot of effort into a job you hate. But the baker was only human, and no one can go without sleep or rest or holidays for ever. It was inevitable that sooner or later, the baker would make a mistake.

This is how it happened. One day in early summer, a lady who lived very near the baker took her little niece into the bakery to choose a cake for her tea. The little girl's mummy was rather ill, which was why Anna-Maria was staying with her aunty. It was also why her aunty was trying to be specially nice to the little girl, although, to be honest, that was not always easy. Perhaps it was because she was worried about her mummy, but Anna-Maria was often a very difficult child.

As they stood looking at the wonderful selection of cakes and biscuits, Mrs Biddle (for that was the aunt's name) urged her niece to make her choice.

"I know they *all* look delicious," she said, "but you must choose just one of them. We can always come back tomorrow so that you can try something else."

But Anna-Maria looked at the lovely cakes and scowled.

"I can't see anything I want," she said.

"But darling," cried Mrs Biddle, "there is everything you could imagine here. Look! What about a doughnut? What about a cream horn? Or you could have a chocolate muffin, or a jam slice, or a coconut swirl."

"No," said Anna-Maria. "That's not what I want."

Mrs Biddle tried again.

"A coffee kiss? A currant bun? A cinnamon plait?"

"No," said the little girl.

"What about a slice from one

of these beautiful *big* cakes? There's a lemon sponge. Or look, a cherry loaf. A chocolate-chip log? A carrot cake? A double-decker date and walnut wonder?"

But Anna-Marie frowned again and shuffled her shoes.

"I don't like anything here," she muttered sullenly.

Mrs Biddle had plenty of patience. She needed it all now.

"Well, what *do* you like?" she asked. "The baker may well have some other cakes at the back, where we can't see them."

"Yes, that's true," smiled the baker. "What would the little lady really like?"

Mrs Biddle had told the baker about Anna-Maria's mother, so he too wanted to be kind to the little girl.

And Anna-Maria did know just what she wanted.

"I'd like a gingerbread man, please," she said, quite politely.

The busy baker's chubby cheeks looked a little pink.

"I'm very sorry," he said. "I'm afraid I haven't made any of those for a long time. My new ginger-

bread teddy bears rather took over, you know. Wouldn't you like one of those?"

"No, thank you," said Anna-Maria. "It has to be a gingerbread man, please."

"Well, I haven't any now," said the smiling baker, "but I will make some tonight specially for you. They will be ready first thing in the morning."

For the first time, Anna-Maria smiled. "Oh, *thank* you!" she cried. "That will be lovely!"

What neither Mrs Biddle nor the baker knew was that the little girl's mother made her gingerbread men on special occasions. Anna-

Maria thought that perhaps she would not miss her mummy quite so much if she had a gingerbread man just like the ones she loved at home.

That night, the busy baker had to work even harder than usual, and perhaps that is why he didn't pay quite as much attention to what he was doing as he should have done.

The next morning, Mrs Biddle and her niece called at the shop only five minutes after it had opened for the day.

"Here you are, sweetheart," smiled the busy baker. "Six little gingerbread men, just for you."

Anna-Maria looked down at the little biscuits in their special box. They were lovely, but her face fell as she glanced at them.

"What's the matter, darling?" asked Mrs Biddle. "Is there something wrong?"

The little girl looked up with tears in her eyes.

"They haven't got any buttons!" she said.

"What? Let me look!" cried the baker, taking back the box. "Oh dear, oh dear, you are quite right. They really *should* have buttons, shouldn't they?"

"Currant buttons," said Anna-Maria firmly.

"Yes, yes, that's just what I was thinking," said the baker, looking a little embarrassed. "I'm so sorry. If you come back tomorrow, I'll make sure I have gingerbread men with buttons. I was thinking of three buttons. Would that be right?"

"That would be just right," said Anna-Maria, for her mother's special gingerbread men always had three currant buttons.

That night, the baker worked hard again. In fact, he was so busy making sure there were buttons on his biscuits that the bread was left to rise for too long and almost burst out of the oven.

Next morning, Anna-Maria and

her aunty were waiting outside the shop when the baker opened the door.

"I've got them right here," he smiled. "And I counted the buttons very carefully."

Anna-Maria's blue eyes were bright as she peered into the box. There was a little smile on her lips. But suddenly her eyes clouded and she almost looked ready to cry.

"Whatever is it now?" asked Mrs Biddle. "They look lovely to me, sweetheart."

"But they don't have red smiley mouths," said Anna-Maria.

It was perfectly true. The jolly gingerbread men had little currant eyes and little currant buttons, but in his concern to make sure there were exactly three buttons on each little man, the busy baker had completely forgotten about the red smiley mouths made from cherries.

"Oh dear," said the baker, "I'm not doing very well for you, am I, my dear? Let me have one last try. Come back tomorrow and I promise I'll have the smiliest gingerbread men you have ever seen. Will you do that?"

"All right," said Anna-Maria. She wanted those gingerbread men so very badly, but she couldn't bring herself to tell her aunty or the baker why.

The day had started badly for the baker, and it didn't improve when his regular customers started to complain about the bread he had allowed to rise for too long.

"It's just not up to your usual high standard," said the Mayor, brushing crumbs off his waistcoat. "What's the trouble? Anything I can help with?"

"No," cried the baker. "Just a silly problem last night. Nothing I can't deal with, I promise you. It won't happen again."

But that night, the baker was so tired that he could hardly tell *what* he was doing. The only thing he could think of was Anna-Maria's sad little face.

He finished his other baking as quickly as he could (and perhaps he didn't take quite as much care as usual), then cleared his table so that he could concentrate all his efforts on the gingerbread men. This time, they must be absolutely perfect.

Soon six little gingerbread men were sitting on a baking tray, ready to go into the oven. They had one smiley cherry mouth. They had two little currant eyes. They had three currant buttons in a row down their tummies. They were just right.

With a sigh of relief, the busy baker popped the little biscuits into the oven and sat down.

He was exhausted! Slowly, his eyelids began to droop. His head began to nod. In less than a minute, he fell fast asleep at his bakery table.

Meanwhile, in the oven, the gingerbread men turned a lovely golden brown. But the busy baker slept on. The gingerbread men began to look a little toasted around their toes. But the busy baker's eyes didn't open. The

buttons on the gingerbread men's tummies began to sizzle, until they turned into little black cinders. But the busy baker didn't stir. Soon the smell of burnt gingerbread filled the bakery, and it was joined by the smell of burnt bread and burnt cakes and burnt biscuits. As the smell drifted across the bakery and tickled the baker's nose, he *jumped* out of his chair with a mighty shout.

"My bread!" he cried, flinging open the oven door. "My cakes! My biscuits! My gingerbread men!"

Everything looked dreadful. The busy baker couldn't imagine that even the ducks on the village pond would want to peck at his burnt offerings.

In despair, the baker glanced at the clock. It was almost seven o'clock in the morning. There was no time to make anything now.

The baker felt bad about his bread and cakes and biscuits. He knew how disappointed all his customers would be. But most of all, he felt awful about the little girl who was pinning her hopes on six smiley gingerbread men.

Anna-Maria wasn't waiting when the busy baker opened his shop door that morning, although several other villagers were. They stared in disbelief as the baker pinned up a notice. Within minutes, news of the bakery disaster was all over the village.

No Bread   No Cakes   No Biscuits

TODAY

Normal service resumes tomorrow.

No one felt angry with the baker. They all knew how hard he worked. They just felt very worried. What if he became really ill? And all because he always tried to do his best for his customers? Before the morning was over, the Mayor had called an Extraordinary Meeting, and everyone in the village (except the baker himself, who was sitting sadly in his empty shop) was trying to think of an idea that would help to make sure the poor man never became so tired again.

Things began to improve for the baker in the afternoon. And what had started off as the worst day of his life, soon became the very best.

At two o'clock, a little face peeped round the shop door. The baker hardly recognised it, because it had the sunniest smile he had ever seen. It was Anna-Maria, and holding her hand was a lady smiling just as broadly. The baker knew at once that it must be the little girl's mother. Their smiles were so alike.

"This is my mummy," said Anna-Maria. "She is better now and has come to take me home. And she brought me a present. I thought you might like one, because I heard what happened last night."

The little girl held out a gingerbread man, made by her own dear mummy. It was rather wobbly looking, and its smile was crooked, but the baker could see that Anna-Maria thought it was the best gingerbread man in the world. And she was right.

Just then, a group of villagers arrived at the door.

"We've come to help," they said. "You need some assistants, and we are going to take turns. We can start at once."

"Hurray!" the baker mumbled ... with his mouth full!

The Mouse's House

NOW THERE are those who enjoy keeping their things clean and tidy and there are those who don't. You can tell as soon as you step inside someone's front door which kind of home you are visiting. Of course, it is nice not to have to move piles of books and papers before you sit in a chair. And no one wants to find their plate covered in a thick layer of dust, but some people are *so* clean and tidy that it's no fun at all to pay them a visit. The Mouse was like that, as you will see.

The Mouse lived in a very cosy little tree-trunk house in the middle of Mendlesham Wood. She probably had been given a proper name when she was a baby, but everyone just called her "Mouse".

Mouse had always been proud of her home, and she had never been untidy. She liked everything to look just right, so that none of the other animals in Mendlesham wood could point their paws at her and say, "Have you *seen* the cobwebs in *her* house?"

But to begin with, Mouse was no more worried about dirt and dust than any moderately houseproud animal in the wood. The change was very gradual. For a long time, she swept her front steps once a day. Then you might sometimes see her,

especially in autumn, giving them a little extra sweep in the afternoon. By the time of this story, she was out on those steps half a dozen times a day.

"It's these horrible old leaves," she would say, if a friend protested that she was working too hard.

"But Mouse, you live in a *tree*!" the friend would say. "Of course there will be leaves."

"Not on my steps there won't!" replied Mouse stoutly, picking up her broom again.

Well, Mouse became as particular about the inside of her house as she was about her front steps. She was constantly dusting and sweeping and washing and wiping. She was a great plumper-up of cushions, too, and she had a hatred of spiders and their webs that would have been funny if it hadn't been rather worrying too.

"Out of my way," Mouse would say to a guest who had come to tea. "I saw one of those pesky little animals run under your chair. I can't rest until I've found him. The very thought of those eight muddy feet running over my floorboards makes me shiver and shake. Watch out! Don't spill your tea!"

It soon became something of a lottery to visit Mouse. You might have a perfectly lovely time, but on her worst days, Mouse was not a good hostess.

"Excuse me, but *did* you wipe your feet as you came in?" she would ask, peering suspiciously at your shoes. "Perhaps you wouldn't mind doing it again."

Then, after you had dutifully wiped them up and down several times on the doormat, Mouse would make a big point of shaking the mat itself outside the door. Of course, that might mean that she felt the step needed sweeping as well. So you see what I mean, conversation at Mouse's tea parties was often a little strained.

Gradually, the animals in

Mendlesham Wood became quite worried about Mouse.

"It isn't healthy to be so finicky," said the owl, whose own home was really none too clean. "Mouse is making herself ill worrying about things that don't matter at all. Why, when I visited her the other day, she told me I couldn't sit in the chairs because I'd flatten the cushions. I mean, what are chairs *for*? That's what I'd like to know."

"It was the same when I called to collect her grocery money," said the rabbit who lived under the old oak tree. "She wouldn't let me knock at the front door in case my paws were dirty. She was peering out of the window, waiting for me, so that she could catch me before I touched it!"

"That's dreadful," said the hedgehog. "Doesn't she know that a little bit of dirt is *good* for you. That's what I always tell my little ones."

Some of the others coughed and looked away. They knew very

well that the hedgehog and her little ones were never invited to Mouse's house because it was well known by everyone that they had *fleas*. Mouse hated fleas almost as much as she hated spiders. Just because they hopped instead of scurrying, it didn't mean that their feet were clean. Very few tiny creatures were welcome in Mouse's home, although she did have a soft spot for moths, for some reason.

"Someone should talk to her," said the owl. "A close friend, I mean," he went on hurriedly, "not someone like me who is really only an acquaintance."

"The sad thing is that she really

doesn't *have* any close friends any more," said the squirrel. "It is so uncomfortable to visit her now that nobody wants to do it. And it's hard to be close friends with an animal you hardly ever see. I can't remember the last time I visited Mouse's house, in fact. I miss having her as a friend."

"I think you're right," said the woodpecker. "I haven't seen her since I made that little attic window at the back for her a few years ago. She complained about the sawdust then, but she was nothing like so fussy as she is now. I don't think she could bear anyone to touch her house in any way."

The animals were well
meaning, but they couldn't really
think of any way to help Mouse. In

the end, it was a complete stranger who made a difference.

That winter was particularly cold. Even the trees shuddered as a howling, icy wind whistled around their roots and branches, frosting their twigs and chilling every little creature who lived nearby. All the animals huddled in their homes, doing the best they could to keep warm.

Mouse had a snugger home than most, especially as she always made sure that her window frames were free from draughts and her strong, tree-trunk walls were free from cracks.

But Mouse didn't like the way

that frost made her windows look dirty, and snow had a habit of dropping from the branches above and falling with an alarming *plop!* on to her steps.

It was on a particularly cold and blustery night that Mouse had an unexpected visitor. She was sitting in front of her fire, sipping a cup of apple tea, when she heard a little squeal outside and then a hammering at her door. Mouse tried to ignore it at first, but then the dreadful thought occurred to her that someone might actually be damaging her home. She pulled her shawl around her shoulders and opened the door.

Outside was a truly pitiful sight. A little mouse, no bigger than Mouse herself, was shivering on the doorstep.

"Please," he said, "could I come in to warm myself for a moment? I won't trouble you for long."

Mouse hesitated for just a second. She thought with horror of the mouse's wet little paws scampering across her sitting room. She shuddered at the thought of his cold, wet little body sitting on one of her chairs. She could imagine the way that he would shake his whiskers all over her carefully polished table. But Mouse could not bear to see another creature suffer, so she stood back from the door.

"Do come in," she said. "Er … the door mat is just here."

"Thank you so much," shivered the stranger mouse, as he stood in the middle of Mouse's sitting room. "I don't think I could have lasted much longer out there. It's no night for a mouse to be out."

"No, indeed," agreed Mouse. "Er … can I take your … er … coat?" She didn't really think that was the right word for the ragged, shapeless garment that the mouse held tightly around himself. But the mouse seemed to know what she meant and handed her the thin, wet cloth.

"I've been travelling for a long time," he said. "I'm on my way to see someone very special, but winter has been harder than I ever thought it would be. I should probably have put off my journey until the spring, but I was so eager to meet this person that I couldn't wait."

Mouse handed the stranger a towel to dry his whiskers before he shook them any more, but the visitor didn't seem to understand and wrapped the towel around his shoulders instead.

"Thank you again," he said. "I should introduce myself. My name is George."

The name sounded vaguely

familiar to Mouse, but she couldn't think why.

"My name is Mouse," she said. "It sounds strange, I know, but I think it's what I've always been called. I can't remember when I was a baby."

George nodded and sat down in the chair. Thankfully the towel was between him and the uphol-stery. Goodness knew when he had last taken a bath.

The newcomer was still shivering, so Mouse hurried to her neat little kitchen and made up a tray of hot soup, bread and juniper biscuits.

"I wasn't expecting visitors,"

she said, apologising for the makeshift supper. And all of a sudden she wondered why that was. There had been a time when her friends visited her every day, but she couldn't remember now the last time that anyone had dropped in.

George didn't find the supper disappointing at all. He was already finishing the soup and stuffing a rather large piece of bread into his mouth.

"This is wonderful," he said, between chews. "I haven't had anything to eat since the day before yesterday."

Mouse was horrified to hear

this. In fact, she was so concerned that she didn't notice until it was too late that George had put his hot soup bowl down on her polished table. She snatched it up with a cry. Sure enough, there was a white ring where the bowl had stood.

"Ooops, sorry," said George.

Mouse knew that she could not possibly send her visitor out into the blizzard again tonight. She hurried upstairs and made sure that the sheets on the spare-room bed were aired. She slipped a hot water bottle into the bed and ran back downstairs again to try to stop George doing any more damage to her furniture. She was too late.

"I am ever so sorry," said George. "I don't know how it happened. One minute I was rocking myself gently in your chair and the next minute the leg fell off. It must have been a little loose, I think."

"Rocking?" said Mouse faintly. She looked up at the wall, and sure enough she could see the mark where the chair had been bumped over and over again. This mouse would bring her home down about her ears if he carried on at this rate!

Nevertheless, Mouse clenched her paws and asked George if he would like a bath before bed.

"That would be bliss," said

George. "I haven't had a bath since…"

"Yes, yes, that's all right," said Mouse hurriedly. She really didn't feel she could cope with the news George had been about to give her.

Five minutes later, Mouse, doing her best to tidy up downstairs, heard George singing at the top of his voice. It was a very silly song, and he wasn't remotely in tune, but still she caught herself smiling. It was such a long time since she had heard anyone really enjoying themselves in her house.

But Mouse's smile was not in place for long. She began to wonder what state the bathroom would be in when George had finished, and just then … *splosh!* … a drop of water bounced off her nose.

Mouse looked up in horror. There was no doubt about it, water was dripping through her beautiful ceiling and on to her sofa below.

Mouse hurried up the stairs and banged furiously on the bathroom door.

"W-w-w-what?" came a voice, after a moment. "Oh no! Oh, I am sorry. I dozed off for a moment and left the taps running. There's not much water on the floor though. Honestly, there isn't."

"That's because it's on the floor downstairs," muttered Mouse to herself, but she felt sorry for the little mouse who was so tired he had almost drowned himself.

A moment later, George appeared at the bathroom door, wearing a pair of Mouse's late father's pyjamas. He looked clean and scrubbed, but his eyelids were drooping, and he had one paw on the door frame to support himself as he said goodnight to his hostess.

"Goodnight," said Mouse. "I hope you sleep well."

It took Mouse another three hours to finish clearing up the sitting room *and* the bathroom, but then her standards were very high. She was exhausted herself when she finally tottered up the stairs to bed. And that is why she fell asleep the moment her head touched the pillow and didn't wake up at the crack of dawn as usual in the morning.

In fact, Mouse woke up feeling rather happy with the world. It took a few seconds for her to realise that this was because the smell of a fried breakfast and freshly brewed acorn coffee was wafting up the stairs.

Mouse sat up in bed. Someone was in her kitchen! Then the events of the night before came flooding back. Oh no! *George* was in her kitchen, and what was more, he was *cooking*!

Mouse flew out of bed and into her dressing gown. Her little feet hardly touched the stairs as she rushed towards the kitchen. One glimpse was enough to tell her that it was even worse than she had feared. There was George, his whiskers singed, flapping a tea towel at a flaming pan, while water running into the sink overflowed on to the floor. A second glimpse showed her two broken cups and a fish slice bent in two. And surely that wasn't … oh no, it couldn't be … that wasn't a *pancake* stuck to the ceiling? Mouse had to sit down in a hurry, and the floor was the nearest place.

"Oh, there you are," called George cheerfully. "I was just making you a little breakfast to thank you for being so kind. If you just wait there while I deal with this little fire, it will be ready for you in just a minute."

Mouse put her head in her hands. George was going to have to go, and he was going to have to go *soon.* She felt that every second that George spent in her house was another opportunity for disaster to strike.

But just at that moment, the visitor pushed a plate of pancakes and syrup under her nose. Much to Mouse's surprise, it smelt *delicious*! With all the excitement the night before, she remembered, she hadn't had any supper herself. Now she was too hungry to do anything other than pick up a spoon and start eating. And the pancakes tasted as delicious as they looked. How extraordinary!

As she munched her way through the pancakes, Mouse became aware that her visitor was talking.

"… so that's why I felt I just had to come and see her," he was saying. "I've heard so many stories about how kind she is to everyone, and how animals flock to see her when they are in trouble. Aunt Petunia sounds such a wonderful person. I don't suppose you know her, do you? She lives somewhere around here. In fact, I'm sure you two must be friends, for you are just as kind as she is. *Do* you know her, Mouse?"

Mouse had the strangest feeling in her tail and whiskers. Petunia! That was a name she hadn't heard for so long. For the first time in years, Mouse knew what her real name was. No wonder George had looked and sounded familiar. He was her own sister Salvia's son.

If Mouse hadn't been sitting down already, she would have done so now. Instead, she asked George if she could have some of his acorn coffee.

Huddled in her dressing gown,
Mouse sipped the excellent coffee
and thought hard. There *had* been a
time when she cared more for
others than for herself. What had
happened? Mouse looked around her

home. In recent years, she had cared more for cleaning and tidying than for anything that was really important. Mouse felt ashamed. How could she confess who she was to this eager young mouse, when the evidence was all too plain that she only ever thought about her perfect home.

Then Mouse began to laugh. The evidence wasn't plain at all! Her kitchen was in ruins. The sitting room ceiling was soggy. There were marks on the walls and furniture, and she hadn't even looked to see what George had done to the spare room.

Mouse looked again at her

nephew. He was certainly a wonderful cook. He just needed a little
guidance about safety and damage
control. Mouse felt warmed by the
idea that George might have to stay
for a few weeks, months or even
years, so that she could help him.

For the first time in ages,
Mouse felt really happy, and that
made her laugh too, especially as the
flood on the floor was now creeping
up her dressing gown.

"George," she smiled, "there's
quite a lot I need to tell you…"

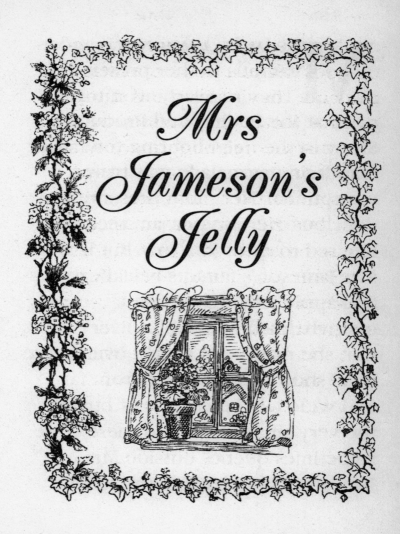

Mrs Jameson's Jelly

Mrs Janice Jameson was famous for her preserves. They regularly won top prize at the Poultry and Produce Show in the neighbouring town. Her mandarin marmalade was truly exceptional. Her plum preserve was delicious. Her juniper jam received five red rosettes in a row. But it was Mrs Jameson's famous blackberry and apple jelly that really overwhelmed her public. Every jar that she made was fought over in the local shop. Visitors came from far and wide for the chance of buying the very smallest jar, and there were sometimes queues outside Mrs Jameson's house when the telltale

smell of simmering fruit wafted out of her windows.

Now Mrs Jameson was quite rightly proud of her jam-making achievements, and she enjoyed the praise of her friends and neighbours, but eventually their appreciation went to head — with rather disastrous consequences.

One day, Mrs Jameson was asked to give a lecture on preserving to the local branch of the Ladies' Luncheon Club. It was quite an honour to be asked, and Mrs Jameson felt a flutter of nervousness as she stood up to give her speech. But she need not have worried. As soon as she embarked upon her favourite subject, her anxiety left her.

Mrs Jameson gave her spellbound audience the benefit of her expertise on Selecting Fruits, Choosing a Preserving Pan, The Art of Stirring, Pots and Their Problems, Sinking Fruit: the Sloppy Simmerer's Curse, and Lovely Labelling. She held her listeners' attention so thoroughly that she began to feel as though no problem of preserving was so great she could not solve it.

"Now I will answer questions," she said grandly. "Who would like to begin?"

One or two ladies timidly put up their hands and voiced their own little difficulties. Mrs Janice Jameson dealt with these in brisk terms. She told one lady that her fruit was substandard and advised another to give up jam-making altogether, as she clearly had not the first idea about it. Other questions were dealt with in an equally robust way, and Mrs Jameson's audience began to be a little restless. Finally, a very superior-looking lady in an enormous hat gave a little laugh.

"It's delightful to know that such quaint old-fashioned hobbies are still being practised," she said. "Of course, those of us that have important work to do simply cannot find the time for such charming pursuits — even if we wanted to."

There was something in her tone that immediately annoyed Mrs Jameson. She felt that she did work as important as any you could mention. How dare the woman in the hat use such a patronising tone?

"I'm quite sure," she replied, "that any lady who is doing truly important work will have the intelligence and diligence to organise her time in such a way that she can pursue any hobby."

"But everyone has their limits, Mrs Jameson," persisted the lady in the hat in a silky voice.

"Nonsense," cried the speaker. "Such talk is for the fainthearted. Why, despite my numerous speaking engagements, I find time to make any amount of blackberry and apple jelly each and every year."

"Any amount?" queried the lady in the hat.

"Any amount," confirmed Mrs Jameson, who recognised a challenge when she heard one.

"In that case," continued her interrogator, "would you be willing to undertake to fill any empty jars that are brought to you? We would pay for your perfect preserves, of course."

"Certainly," said Mrs Jameson.

She thought quickly. Every year when she came to make her jelly there was a shortage of jars. This year was likely to be no exception. It simply was not possible that local people could find so many jars that Mrs Jameson could not fill them.

Mrs Jameson smiled sweetly at the lady in the hat. "Perhaps you would like to come and watch," she

said. "I'm sure you have a great deal to learn."

Oh dear, Mrs Jameson had made an enemy, and that is never a wise thing to do if you can help it. But she was very confident of her abilities. Making jelly came as naturally to Janice Jameson as sitting in front of the television does to most people. She could not wait to roll up her sleeves and go to work.

The next morning, when Mrs Jameson opened her front door, she found a cardboard box with thirty-two empty jars inside. She laughed scornfully.

"I can make thirty-two jars of jelly before breakfast," she cried, not entirely accurately.

Ten minutes later, Mrs Jameson was on the telephone to her favourite niece.

"Leonora!" she trilled. "Your services are needed. Please go out this morning and pick as many blackberries as you can find. I shall pay my usual rates."

"No problem, Aunty," said Leonora, who had heard from a

friend's mother about the Great Jelly Challenge and felt sure that her money box would gain from it.

That morning, Leonora went out and picked ten whole baskets of blackberries. She knew where the juiciest berries were to be found and was careful not to scratch her hands as she picked.

Back at home, Mrs Jameson sent her husband out to pick apples from the orchard.

"Only the best ones," she warned him.

"Yes, dear," said Mr Jameson, who had endured various tasks connected to his wife's hobby over the years.

By midday, Mrs Jameson had everything she needed. It was time to begin.

For the next few hours, the kitchen was full of delicious bubbling sounds. Mrs Jameson washed and peeled. She cored and chopped, and simmered and stirred. Finally, the moment of truth arrived. Mrs Jameson put a spoonful of jelly on a cold saucer and waited to see if it would set.

"Perfect!" cried Mrs Jameson, and she set about straining her jelly into jars.

By teatime, thirty-two jars of blackberry and apple jelly were standing on the kitchen table.

Thirty-two lids had been sealed, and thirty-two labels had been written (in Mr Jameson's best handwriting). Mrs Jameson felt tired but triumphant.

But next morning, when she opened her front door, she found another cardboard box of empty jars. This time there were sixty-four of them!

Mrs Jameson felt a little faint, but she was not going to give up. Summoning her troops (otherwise known as Leonora and Mr Jameson), she set to work once more. And by the end of the day, all sixty-four jars were filled, lidded and labelled.

There was no room on the

kitchen table for the new batch of
jam, so Mrs Jameson carefully
stacked the jars back in the cardboard box they had come in. Then
she wrote "This way up" in big black
letters on the box to prevent a sticky
accident.

You can guess what happened
the next morning. Over a hundred
jars stood on Mrs Jameson's
doorstep. She rose to the challenge,
of course, but I have to say that she
did not set about jelly-making that
day with her usual enthusiasm. In
fact, the troops were a little jaded as
well.

"I've picked all the best
berries," Leonora complained.

"Then you'll have to go farther afield," said her aunt. "I can't have substandard berries in my jelly."

Mr Jameson protested too. "My writing hand is aching," he said. "I think I may have done it a permanent injury."

"How do you think my wrists

feel," demanded his wife, "with all that stirring and straining? Yes, straining is the word, I can tell you. The honour of our household is at stake. We must go on!" she finished dramatically.

Mr Jameson climbed reluctantly into the apple trees again. There were very few fruits left that were worth picking.

Mrs Jameson put on a clean apron and got to work. It was very late when she finished, but every jar was filled with jelly, and it is a tribute to the tired cook's high standards that the first jar tasted just as good as the last.

Mrs Jameson went to bed,

confident that there could be no more spare jars in the whole area. It simply was not possible. Still, the next morning she opened the front door very gingerly.

It was a nightmare. There must have been at least five hundred jars standing on the step. Mrs Jameson had to sit down at the bottom of the stairs. In her heart of hearts, she knew that she could not fill five hundred jars, but she telephoned her niece all the same.

"No," said Leonora. "No, no, a thousand times no!"

"Double rates?" pleaded her aunt desperately.

"No!"

"Triple?"

"No!" And Leonora rather rudely put the phone down.

Mr Jameson's reaction was much the same.

"I'm only human, dear," he said. "I can't make apples appear on the trees. You've done your best. After all, you're only human too."

How Mrs Janice Jameson regretted her boastful words to the Ladies' Luncheon Club. How she wished she had known, as a friend helpfully told her at least three days too late, that the lady in the hat owned the biggest jam-jar factory in the entire country. Mrs Jameson felt that she never wanted to see another jam jar in her life.

At least the local shop had plentiful supplies of blackberry and apple jelly that year, but it was the last time it was to appear on the shelves. For Mrs Janice Jameson has sold her saucepans and taken up … knitting!

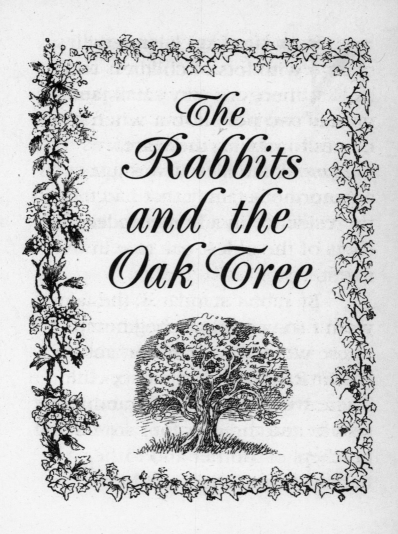

The
Rabbits
and the
Oak Tree

Now there are large families, with lots of children, and there are very small families of only two people, but when it comes to rabbits, there are *enormous* families. It was just such an enormous family that had taken up residence in a home under the roots of the oldest oak tree in the forest.

By rabbit standards, the family wasn't so very big to begin with. There were Mother Rabbit and Father Rabbit with their six children. There were two sets of grandparent rabbits and three or four sisters and brothers of Mother and Father Rabbit — *and* their children.

Altogether, there must have been about thirty lively little rabbits.

The oak tree had lived in the forest for hundreds of years. Its roots were thick and twisted. As soon as he saw them, Father Rabbit knew that he could dig a very fine home among those roots, and that is exactly what he did. And the oak tree didn't seem to mind.

But over the next few years, the rabbit family didn't so much grow as *explode*! The children had children, and the children's children had children. Very soon there were over two hundred rabbits living under the oldest oak tree in the forest.

Of course, some expansion had been necessary. You can't squeeze more and more rabbits into a small space (unless you are a conjuror). So Father Rabbit and his brothers and cousins and nephews dug more and more passages and rooms among the roots of the tree. I must say they did it beautifully. There were cosy little bedrooms and spacious sitting rooms. There were places for the baby rabbits to play and quiet spots where the older rabbits could sit and chat and have a little peace.

But as the months passed, the oak tree began to feel worried. It seemed that his roots were not planted so firmly in the soil as they once had been. Where once he had enjoyed feeling the breeze whistling through his leaves, now he felt uneasy and just a little bit wavering and wobbly. Winter was coming, and the oak tree dreaded the gales that sometimes rushed through the wood.

"I don't know what to do," he muttered to the much younger birch tree standing near him.

The birch tree was very flattered. It was usually she who asked the ancient oak tree for advice. She rustled her branches and thought as hard as possible.

"I'm sure those rabbits don't mean to do you harm," she said. "The trouble is that it's not easy for a tree to talk to a rabbit. They just don't speak the same kind of language. What you need is an interpreter. Someone who can understand both sides."

"By Jove, you're right!" cried the oak tree. "And there is only one woodland creature who can do such a thing. We need to find a woodsprite."

You have probably never seen a woodsprite, for they are so small and flit about so quickly that the best you can usually do is to *think* you've caught sight of one out of the corner of your eye. If you have ever noticed a leaf waving more vigorously than its neighbours, or seen the sunshine sparkling on a drop of water as it shimmers on a cobweb, you have probably almost seen a woodsprite. They are very difficult to find.

Luckily, ancient trees know a little of the old magic. The oak tree gave a kind of a rumble and little bit of a creak. It almost sounded as if it was singing. In fact, it was calling to the woodsprites to come to its aid.

In only a few moments, a little creature flitted across the clearing to the oak tree. It could have been a dried leaf, drifting in the breeze. It could have been a butterfly, alighting on a branch. It could have been a clump of fluffy dandelion seeds, floating through the air. But it wasn't. It was a woodsprite, answering the call of the mighty oak tree.

It did not take the tree long to explain the problem.

The woodsprite nodded her head and flitted down one of the holes at the base of the tree. She travelled through tunnel after tunnel, until, as luck would have it, she came face to face with Father Rabbit, who was munching his dinner.

"Hello," said the rabbit politely. "How can I help you?"

"I'm very much afraid that you

are damaging the mighty oak above you," said the woodsprite, in a voice that was no louder than a feather falling on to a bed of moss.

"Damaging it? How?" asked the rabbit in surprise. "I thought he quite liked us living here. We feel so safe among his strong roots."

"That's just the problem," explained the woodsprite. "Your burrows have loosened the roots so much that the oak tree fears the next strong wind could cause him to fall.

"Well," said the rabbit slowly, "I don't mean to sound uncaring, but all trees must fall sometime, and the oak tree has reached a very great age."

"And could reach an even greater one," said the woodsprite. "And what do you think will happen if the tree *does* fall? Its roots will come tearing out of the ground, destroying your home and leaving your burrows open, so that any passing fox or owl could carry off your little ones."

"When you put it like that," said the rabbit, "I can see that it is our duty to help the noble tree. But it seems to me that the only way we can help is to move altogether, and leave our beautiful home."

"No, no," said the sprite. "Not ten minutes from here is a lovely patch of heath, with sandy soil and thorny bushes above. It is the perfect spot for you to dig a new home, and you will be much safer there. And if you fill in most of the burrows in this home, you could keep a smaller, holiday home here to visit in turns whenever you need a break."

That sounded an excellent idea, so the rabbit hopped off to

call a family meeting to discuss the matter.

A couple of hours later, the oak tree felt a squiggly, wriggly feeling around his roots, as the rabbits started to fill in a large number of their burrows and bedrooms. Before nightfall, the tree felt much happier than he had done for weeks. His roots gripped the soil firmly, and he could allow his branches to wave without feeling that he was about to topple over. He gave a happy sigh and settled down to grow for another five hundred years or so.

Meanwhile, the rabbits were having a wonderful time in the sandy heath. In fact, they enjoyed it so much that they very soon had no wish at all to visit their holiday home under the oak tree.

So do the burrows stand empty, filling up gradually with dried leaves? No, someone has moved in who flits so lightly along the passageways that the oak tree feels his toes are being tickled. Next time you hear an oak tree giggle, don't be surprised. It is simply that a woodsprite is not far away.

The First Christmas Tree

ON A VERY SPECIAL NIGHT, long, long ago, a star shone down upon a stable. Night after night, it shone, until some wise men, travelling from the East, reached the building over which it hovered. They went inside to offer gifts of gold, frankincense and myrrh to the baby they found inside.

Later, the baby and its parents were warned of danger, and they packed their belongings in the night and journeyed on to Egypt. Few people know that the star also continued on its travels, wandering across the dark sky in search of a final resting place.

The star travelled over the

desert, and looked down on mile upon mile of barren sand. As the winds blew, the sand was constantly shifted from place to place, forming mountains and valleys that were never still. That was no place for a star to rest.

As the star journeyed, it crossed the ocean. Far below, the restless waves were in ceaseless motion. Over and over again, they

rose and fell, for the ocean is never at peace. The star could not find a final stopping place on the restless seas.

The star travelled on, and many people looked up into the night sky and pointed at the shining visitor.

"What does it mean? Will it bring us good luck or bad?" they asked each other.

But the star carried no luck. It simply shone by night and became dark by day, always travelling to find a place to stay.

The star travelled over the mountains, as cold and bright in the moonlight as the star itself. On their peaks, the snow lay unchanging, but on the slopes below, it sometimes drifted into heaps and sometimes melted into a fast-flowing river, gushing down the rocky mountain face to the valleys beneath. Even the unchanging mountains endlessly shifted and shrugged, sometimes sending down huge shelves of snow as avalanches. The star could not rest on a mountain top.

On its journey, the star travelled over towns and cities, where lights burned as brightly by night as they did by day. In the orange glow given off by a thousand lamps and candles, the star could hardly be seen. It could not come to rest in such a place as that.

When it came to the great empty wastes of the Arctic, the star believed that it had found a home as pure and changeless as itself. It hovered above the North Pole and saw itself reflected far below in the great sheets of ice that cover the sea. Everything was cold, cold and silent. The star looked down on the earth and felt disconnected and alone. It found that what it sought was peace, not emptiness.

Moving south again, the star came to a great forest. In the moonlight, its trees seemed clothed in dark green robes. Here and there, frost sugared their branches, and tiny creatures huddled to keep warm.

The trees were majestic, straight and tall, and they were growing. With every second that passed, the trees were reaching higher and higher, slowly stretching nearer and nearer to the star. For a long time, the star hovered over the forest, not knowing where to come to rest.

Then, far below, it saw that the trees were beginning to thin. Further south, they did not stand in serried ranks but grew singly, tall and proud. One tree in particular seemed to stand as a bridge between the earth and sky, its roots firmly in the soil, while its topmost branches brushed the stars.

The special star floated gently

above the mighty tree, so that its pure, white light lay cleanly upon the feathery branches. This was the place where it would stay, in touch with all above and below.

At Christmas time, when we remember the baby in the stable and the star that shone, night after night, above the poor building, many people bring a fir tree into their homes and place a silver star at its very top. It is a reminder that the star of the first Christmas, although it was far too high and heavenly to be reached by people on earth, still shed light into their lives, and came to rest with all the living things here below.

The King of the Forest

ONCE UPON A TIME, there was a King who loved trees. Ever since he was a baby Princeling, when his nurse put him out in his crib to look up at the green leaves of a mighty oak waving above him, he had loved all living things. But trees made his heart sing and his eyes grow misty. He thought they were the most beautiful things in the world.

When he was a boy, the King climbed every tree he could find. From high in the branches, he could almost feel that he was part of the tree, swaying in the wind, warm in the summer sunshine. He wished that he could live there for ever, and often spent the night in a little treehouse built for him by the Royal Carpenter. There he could forget he was a Prince and pretend to be like other children. For Princes are brought up to know that they will one day have the terrible responsibility of being King. Some Princes cannot wait to sit upon the throne,

but others long for a quiet life, doing the things they love.

The hero of this story was just like that. If he had had his way, he would have stayed all day among his beloved trees, far away from the busy world of life at court.

However, the day came, as everyone expected, when the old King died. The new King wept for his father and for himself, for he felt that his freedom was over.

No longer could the new King wander in the woods he loved. He had to sit in his palace, reading documents and listening to the requests of his subjects.

Not all of the work was

boring. The King enjoyed helping people who needed his aid, and some of the pageants and processions were very impressive, but he had no time to walk beneath the shady boughs or tend the oak trees around the palace.

One day, however, as he looked at an ancient map of his kingdom, he noticed a large area of green at the very edge of his realm.

"What is that?" he asked his Chief Minister.

"That, Sire, is an ancient wood, planted by your great-great-great-great-great-great-great-great grandfather. Most of it has been cut down now, which is why you do not see it on more modern maps of our beloved country."

"So when you say my great-great-whatever planted it...," the King began.

"Of course, Sire, I mean that he instructed that it should be planted. He didn't go out there himself. Ha ha! No, no, royal workers planted the trees under royal instructions." The King felt happier than he had at any time since he came to the throne.

"This," he said, "is a custom that I feel is worth reviving. We shall plant a new royal forest, and it will bigger and better than any forest ever planted."

Despite his busy workload, over the next few months, the King somehow managed to find time to supervise every detail of the plans for the new forest. It was going to be magnificent.

"I should like planting to begin immediately," he said, when the site had been chosen. "Send the Chief Forester to me."

But the Chief Forester looked very worried when the King outlined his plans.

"I don't think that will be possible, Sire," he said.

"Not possible?" cried the King. "Why ever not? We have the men. We have the land."

"But we don't have the plants, Sire," said the Chief Forester. "We will need thousands and thousands, no, probably millions and millions of little oak tree plants, and there are not that number to be had in this kingdom or the next. Indeed, I am sure that there are not so many baby trees of the right kind to be found in the whole world."

The King paused. There was no doubt in his mind that his Chief Forester was absolutely right. Why had he not thought of it before? Would his great plan have to be abandoned after all?

"Let me think about it," said the King, "and come to see me at the same time tomorrow. This will be an extraordinary forest. We shall need an extraordinary plan."

All night long, the King tossed and turned. He was determined that his forest would be planted.

"I need this forest," he muttered to himself. "The people need this forest. The King's forest. The people's forest. *The people's forest!*" That was it! The King fell into a deep and peaceful sleep.

Next morning, the King could hardly wait for his Chief Forester to arrive. When he did, the King explained his plan. The Forester's eyes widened, but he was smiling. It would work!

Losing no time, the King called for a proclamation to be sent to every part of his realm.

ALL SUBJECTS

are invited to

PLANT AN ACORN

for the Royal Forest

Full instructions given.

Your tree could live for a thousand years!

It was a wonderful idea. There was hardly a person in the kingdom who didn't plant a little acorn in a pot, or a jar, or a cup. Tiny children of two years old planted them. Venerable old gentlemen of ninety-two planted them. All anybody could talk about, wherever you went, was how well their acorns were growing. The newspapers gave advice on the best growing conditions. Magazines devoted whole articles to the best way to talk to your acorn, for one of the greatest gardeners in the land had announced that all plants do better if they are talked to regularly. Another magazine suggested songs that could be sung to the acorns, while yet another actually asked a composer to write a special acorn song.

Soon, little shoots began to appear, then two little leaves. After two years, sturdy little oak tree plants stood on the doorstep of every house in the land.

At last, the Great Planting could begin.

It took five hundred men a whole year to plant the forest. After that, a hundred men tended the small plants and watched them grow into slender saplings.

Well, that was long ago, but the forest still stands. Now, not only the King but all his people can walk proudly under the majestic trees and say to their children, "Your great-great-great-great grand-father (or grandmother!) planted one of these trees."

The people love the forest almost as much as the King who planted it. Although he died long ago, he is remembered by everyone in the country as the King of the Forest. If he is looking down on it now, he will be weeping for joy — or making plans for another forest of his beloved oak trees!

The
Last
Tree

ONCE UPON A TIME, there was an island covered with trees. They grew so thickly that their branches met overhead. No light from the sun could filter down to the forest floor, so nothing grew there. And as nothing grew except trees, there was also nothing for most small animals and insects to eat. Only a few creatures survived in the topmost branches of the trees, where the sunlight dappled the glossy green leaves.

One day, a scientist came to the island. He examined the trees and the living things that shared the island with them. Then he sent in his report to the ruler of the country that owned the island.

The scientist reported that trees had overrun the island, destroying other plant life and severely restricting the wildlife that could survive there. He advised that exactly half of the trees should be cut down. This would allow light to reach the forest floor. Gradually,

other species would begin to thrive again on the island.

The ruler to whom the report was sent hesitated. He formed several committees to discuss the matter. He set up a special enquiry to look at other parts of the world where similar actions had been taken. He asked another scientist to prepare his own report, to check the findings of the first scientist.

At last, the ruler found that the advice he was receiving from everyone was overwhelming. He ordered that half the trees on the island should be cut down.

It took a long while for the

work to be carried out. There was nowhere on the island that the woodcutters could so much as pitch a tent, so they had to travel to the island each day in a boat. They had only a few hours to work before the boat returned to take them back home to the mainland before nightfall.

When the woodcutters had finished their work, all the fallen trees had to be removed. Once again committees, special enquiries and two scientists suggested suitable methods. In the end, it was a small boy, who had been reading his sister's encyclopedia, who offered the solution. The trees were pushed into the sea and floated on the tide to the mainland.

For several years, no one visited the island. The plan was to leave it undisturbed to see what new kinds of plants and animals would begin to live there. Finally, after seven years, the original scientist returned to the island.

It was a terrible disappointment. Instead of leaving space for new plants to grow, the felling of the trees had given the remaining trees extra space to grow taller themselves. Their branches grew longer, until they touched each other overhead. Just as before, not a single ray of sunlight reached the forest floor. Only the creatures that had survived before the trees were cut down still lived on the island, high in the branches.

The ruler demanded that new studies and new committees should be set up. Another plan was needed for the island. It didn't seem to occur to anyone that the island could simply be left alone.

This time, the advice was more sweeping. All the trees must be cut down to enable other living things to grow on the island.

After the usual committees and enquiries, the plan was carried out. Once again, it was a mammoth task. In fact, this time, the trees were bigger and more difficult to fell. When every single tree was cut down, they were floated away to the nearby mainland as before.

Another seven years passed before a study was carried out. This time, two scientists visited the island together. As they approached it in their boat, they peered at the horizon, looking for signs of life — a fuzz of green over the island, perhaps, or the beating of wings as a flock of birds rose up at their approach. But they found nothing.

That's right. There were no trees. No birds. No insects. No plants. No animals. There were no living things on the island at all. It was dead.

The scientists spent two days searching for even the tiniest sign of life. Finally, they were forced to admit that even seaweed did not grow on the rocks around the shore.

Something had plainly gone wrong. The ruler set up a committee as usual, to find out where mistakes had been made. On the last day of the enquiry, a very important witness came to give his opinion.

This old man was well known as a world authority on islands and the living things that make their homes on them. He was rather frail now, but his mind was as sharp as ever. Everyone waited with interest for his views.

"Is it a fact," he was asked, "that no living things now survive on the island?"

"Yes, that is true," he replied.

"And is it a fact that there are no living things *able* to survive on the island?"

"No," he said, "that is not so."

"So what are these creatures or plants that could do well on so barren a piece of ground?"

The old man looked around at everyone in the room.

Why, trees," he said.

The Woodman's Daughter

ONCE UPON A TIME, there lived a hardworking woodman. All day he was busy in the forest, trimming and felling trees. Once a week, he would load up his cart with wood and set off for the nearest town to sell it. It was a long and tiring journey, and the woodman rarely arrived home before darkness had fallen.

When the woodman was very young, he met a pretty girl on one of his trips to the town. She thought him strong and handsome, and he was bowled over by her loveliness. For a whole year, they met once a week, and both began to long for the days to pass until their next precious meeting.

At last, the woodman plucked up the courage to ask the girl to marry him. To his delight, she agreed, and her father was only too delighted to welcome the hardworking young man into his large family.

"It is a pity you have no brothers!" he joked, looking at his eight remaining daughters.

The wedding was a simple affair, for neither the woodman nor his father-in-law had much money, but you have never seen a happier couple than the pair who left the church together.

If only it had lasted! At first all went well. The newly married couple were only unhappy when they were parted. But the wife began to realise that she must be on her own all day in the lonely forest. She was used to the town, where she could visit her friends or look in shop windows when she was bored. Here there was nothing but trees. The young wife soon began to feel that she hated trees more than anything else on earth.

The woodman could not understand why his wife became sad and silent. He had been brought up to a life in the forest. Nothing was more beautiful to him than an oak tree standing proudly in a glade, its branches outspread to shelter the little creatures who made their homes around it.

However, the young man understood that his wife might miss her family and her old home, so he took her with him each week when he carted his logs into town. The young woman came to long for those days, just as she had longed for them before her marriage.

Then, one day, the woodman's wife told him that she was going to have a child. The woodman was overjoyed. Not only did he long for a son to teach the ways of the woods, but he felt that his wife would be happier with someone to look after all day.

But as the time for the baby's birth drew near, the mother-to-be became more and more quiet and sullen. The woodman felt sure that it was simply that she was tired and longing for her baby to be born.

That week, when the couple went into the nearby town, everything was as usual. The woodman took his wife to her parents' house, while he went to sell his wood.

However, when he returned to collect his wife, he found her father at the door, looking worried and upset.

"I'm sorry, my son," said the old man, "but she refuses to return with you. She insists that she must stay here until the baby is born. Perhaps she is right. A woman should have other women about her at such a time. She will feel differently when it is all over."

The woodman was surprised and unhappy, but he could understand how his young wife might be feeling, so he kissed her gently and left her in the town.

Each week after that, the woodman rushed eagerly to his father-in-law's house to see his wife. And the third time he visited, he was greeted by the wonderful sound of a baby's cry.

The woodman flew upstairs to see his son. His wife was sitting up in bed, the baby beside her in a cradle. The young man hugged and kissed his wife and asked how she was. Then he turned to the cradle and looked down on the most perfect little baby he had ever seen.

"He's beautiful," he breathed, touching one tiny hand. "What shall we call him?"

"I have named her Agnes," said his wife, hardly looking at the child beside her.

The woodman was shocked. "I don't know why, but I was expecting a boy!" he cried. "Well, she is lovely too, of course. And perhaps we shall have a son next time, my dear."

But his wife turned her face away and gazed out of the window with a faraway look.

The woodman could hardly wait to take his family home again. Each week, before he set out for the town, he put flowers in all the rooms and laid the table for two.

But each week, he returned alone to the forest. At first, his wife said that she was tired and unwell from the birth. The woodman was sympathetic and told her to stay as long as she liked with her family.

Later, when his wife was up and about, she said that the baby was too delicate for the long journey. The woodman had no experience of babies. His daughter looked strong and healthy, but he could not be sure. Perhaps it was right that she should stay.

Gradually, weeks turned into months. Soon, it was almost a year since the woodman's wife had come back to live with her family. The young man began to understand in his heart that she would never

return to live with him. His little daughter would grow up outside the forest.

Each week, the woodman went to see his little girl. She seemed to wait eagerly for his visits, and put up her chubby little arms to be hugged.

Now it was the woodman who looked forward to his trips to town once again. They were the highlight of his week.

Then, one day, when the woodman called at his father-in-law's house, the old man met him at the door with a look of shame on his kindly face.

"My daughter is not here," he said. "She left this note for us. It seems that she met a soldier in the town and has gone overseas with him. She slipped out one night. We did not see her go."

The woodman felt as if a knife had stabbed into his heart.

"And my little one?" he gasped.

"Oh, she is here," said the old man. "She will be so happy to see her daddy again."

The woodman ran into the house and scooped up his little daughter in his arms. The tears ran down his weatherbeaten cheeks as he thought how nearly he had lost her.

"I am taking her with me," he said. "She shall live in the forest."

The fond grandfather tried to persuade the woodman not to take the little girl, but his mind was made up.

"I will bring her to see you every week," he promised.

So the little girl went to live

with her father. Every day, he took her with him into the forest, which she grew to love as dearly as her father did.

The years passed, and the little girl grew up. She was the loveliest child you have ever seen. And as time went on, she became a very beautiful young woman indeed.

Now it was the young men of the town who looked forward to the woodman's weekly visit, for his lovely daughter accompanied him. It was not long before she met a young tailor, and found that she liked him very much.

When the tailor shyly approached the woodman to ask for his

daughter's hand, he was not ready for the reception he received. The normally gentle woodman threw him across the street and warned him never to come near his daughter again.

"I cannot bear to lose you," he told his daughter. "And besides, marriages between townsfolk and forestfolk never work out. You must stay at home in future."

Now the woodman did not mean to be unkind, but he was afraid, so afraid, that the girl who had become the centre of his life would be lost to him for ever. In his fear, he could not think or feel properly, and so he made his daughter a prisoner in her home.

But the young girl loved her tailor, and although she loved her father too, she felt a new life calling to her. One day, when her father was at work, she packed her bags and walked the long miles into the town. She and the tailor were married that very day.

When he discovered that his daughter was gone, the woodman was beside himself with grief. He felt that he had lost the only thing in the world that mattered to him.

For the first time in his life, he did not go out into the forest, but lay on his bed and stared blankly at the ceiling. He foresaw day after day of dark loneliness

stretching out ahead. It was too
much to bear.

But as tears stained his pillow,
the woodman heard the sound of a
horse and cart growing nearer.

It was the woodman's daughter
and her new husband.

When he saw his daughter's

happy face, the woodman could not feel angry or sad any more.

"Forgive me," he cried. "I thought I only wanted you to be happy, but I was really only thinking of myself."

"No, no," said the girl, putting her arms around him. "I know that you were worried for me and wanted to keep me safe at home. But my husband is a good man. He will bring me to see you as often as I like, and you shall come to visit us too. We have a beautiful little house, not quite in the town and not quite in the forest, but just where the trees end and the road begins.

Now the woodman cried tears

of joy. He understood that in order to keep something, you sometimes have to let it go free.

The woodman is old now. He no longer goes to the town with his logs, but he looks forward to his daughter's visits. They are the highlight of his week.

Besides, he now has a grandson who takes a great interest in the forest. The woodman is eager to teach the boy all he knows, which makes him very happy.

The Song of Spring

THERE WAS ONCE a little bird who lived in a tree on the edge of a wood. All year long, she was as busy as could be. In spring, she chose a site for her new nest and gathered twigs and moss to build it. Then she laid her eggs and settled down to hatch them.

She only left the eggs for seconds at a time, when she hopped off to find a quick snack. It was during one of these very short breaks that something strange happened in the little bird's nest. When she returned, one of her eggs seemed to have grown bigger!

"That's odd," said the little bird to herself. "It has never happened before." But the egg was the right shape and the right colour. The little bird wondered if she had become so tired sitting on the eggs that she could no longer think properly. She decided to have a quick snooze and settled down comfortably once again.

Day after day, the little bird sat on her nest, keeping the eggs snug and warm.

"Soon I shall hear that first

little *tap tap*," she said to herself. "Then I shall see my darling little children. I can hardly wait."

Sure enough, the little bird woke one morning to a tiny sound under her feathers. *Tap tap! Tap tap!*

Soon a little crack appeared in one of the eggs, and a tiny orange

beak poked through. It was followed by a sleepy little head and a damp little body. Then the new nestling sat quietly in the sun until his feathers dried.

The little bird hardly had time to feel proud of her son before another *tap tap!* came from one of the other eggs. Once again, a little beak was followed by a little bird. Now there were two.

The little bird had to wait until evening for her third egg to hatch. This baby was just as beautiful as the first two.

The mother bird looked at the last egg. It was the largest of all. She listened hard, but could hear no tapping. Surely this egg was not going to be much longer?

One day passed and then another. The little bird did not know what to do. She needed to fly off to find food for her three little nestlings, but she did not like to leave the unhatched egg. At last, there was a very loud *TAP TAP!* and the last egg cracked in two. Out hopped a very strange bird indeed.

The mother bird felt a thrill of fear. She knew exactly what this bird was. It was a *cuckoo*. If she was not careful, it would push her other babies out of the nest.

The baby cuckoo stared at its

mother and opened its beak. It already wanted food.

"All right," said the bird, "I will feed you, but you must promise me not to harm any of my other babies. If you do, I will push *you* right out of the nest. Do you understand me?"

"*Quark*!" The young cuckoo understood very well.

That spring, the mother bird exhausted herself finding food for her brood. At last the day came when they flew away from the nest.

It was sad for the mother, but her heart swelled with pride when she heard a bird singing far away.

"*Cuckoo cuckoo*!"

"That's my boy," she said.

Daisy the Runaway Doll

DAISY FANCIED HERSELF the smartest, the most beautiful, the best dressed, and altogether the most elegant of all the dolls in Laura's room.

For one thing, although everyone called her Daisy, her full name was much grander. It was Daisy Dorinda Deborah Delilah Dinah Darlington Dean. For another thing, there was only one of her — not like some other dolls, who have identical sisters or brothers everywhere you care to look!

No, Daisy was very, very special. She had been handmade by Laura's Aunt Susan, who had given her to Laura for her fourth birthday.

Her eyes were made of shiny black buttons. Her hair was made of the finest sunflower-gold wool. Her smile was sewn on with rosy red thread. She had three beautiful dresses, all with matching shoes and lacy socks. She had her own suitcase for all her finery and her own little blue umbrella. She sat proudly in her own special place on Laura's bed.

Laura took good care of Daisy. Every day she combed her golden hair, dressed her up in one of her beautiful dresses, and took her out in her buggy. Laura took Daisy to the park, to the shops, and to visit friends. Sometimes Laura had tea parties, and Daisy was always the guest of honour. Laura loved Daisy, and Daisy loved Laura, and they were happy together.

Things went on in this pleasant, carefree way for a long time. Then, one summer afternoon, something terrible happened.

A *dog* came to live with Laura and her parents. He was a big, sloppy, floppy-eared, tail-wagging, hairy, muddy-pawed spaniel called Max. And Laura loved *him*, just as she loved Daisy.

It wouldn't have been so bad if Max had stayed out in the garden. But to Daisy's dismay, he was allowed in the house with Laura and her mother and father. Max was even

allowed in Laura's room! And, to
Daisy's horror, he was sometimes
even allowed to jump up on the
bed! Then he would snuffle and
nuzzle Daisy with his big wet nose,
until Laura called him away.

"Come on, Max," Laura would say happily. "Catch the ball!" And she would grab her blue rubber ball and throw it into the air. Max, his ears flying and his tail flapping wildly, would leap into the air and catch the ball in his big, wet mouth. Then he would bound across the room, set the ball at Laura's feet, and wait for her to do it all again.

Max never watched where he was going, and he didn't care who or what was in the way. He often stepped on Laura's cuddly toys with his big clumsy paws. He knocked down her trucks and cars and books with his wagging tail. He crashed into the house where the little tiny dolls lived and knocked it over. And sometimes he picked up Laura's teddy bear and flung him right into the air!

The amazing thing was that neither Laura nor any of the other toys seemed to mind all this madness and mayhem. In fact, they all seemed to *enjoy* playing with Max! But Daisy didn't want any part of his rowdy games, and she always shrank back when she heard Max's bark.

But the more she shrank back, the more Max seemed to want to play with her. "Come on!" he would yap at Daisy. "Please play with me! I'll give you a ride in the air! Old Teddy loves it, and you might too!"

"Go away, you monster!" Daisy would hiss at Max when Laura's back was turned. "Leave me alone! Just leave me alone!"

One morning towards the end of summer, Laura got dressed in some smart new clothes.

"I'm starting school today," she

told Daisy, "so I won't be able to play with you so much. But don't worry. Max will look after you, won't you, Max?"

Right behind her, Max wagged his tail enthusiastically.

Later, when Daisy heard the door close behind Laura and her Mum, she dreaded what would happen next. Any minute now…

"*Woof! Woof!* Who's ready for some fun?" barked Max, as he came hurtling into the room with his floppy ears flying.

"I am! I am!" shouted Old Teddy. "I want to go flying high in the air!"

"We are! We are!" squealed the

little tiny dolls. "Let's play 'Earth-quake' again, Max, where you rattle the dolls' house and make everything wobbly!"

"I'm ready, Max!" called Cuddly Bunny. "Play 'Elephant Steps' on my tummy, Max!"

But Max knew who *he* wanted to play with. He leapt up on to the bed and bounded towards Daisy, the dainty doll.

"Come on, Daisy," he barked, tugging at her arm. "You'll have fun, really!"

"Leave me alone!" snapped Daisy. "Go away, before you mess up my golden hair and tear my beautiful clothes!"

"I'll be careful," barked Max eagerly. "I promise!"

"No," said Daisy, "no, no, NO!"

So Max went off to play with the other toys until Laura came home again.

The same thing happened the next day, and the next. Each morning, Max would jump up on the bed and say, "Please will you play with me today, Daisy?" And each day, Daisy's answer was exactly the same.

"No, no, no. And that is *final*!"

But Max just would not give up, and after several weeks of this, one morning he went too far. He tugged and tugged at Daisy's arm

until he pulled the sleeve of her
beautiful dress right off!

"Now look what you've done!"
shouted Daisy. "That does it. I'm
leaving. I have to go away and find
another home — one without a
dog!"

And with that, Daisy climbed
down from the bed, packed all her
things in her carrying case, and ran
out of the room. A moment later, she
was *thumpety-thumpety-thumpeting*
down the stairs, trailing her case and
her own special blue umbrella
behind her.

"Daisy, wait!" called Max. "What
will Laura say?"

"Come back, Daisy! Come

back!" cried Old Teddy, Cuddly Bunny and the little tiny dolls.

But Daisy was not turning back. She ran into the living room, clambered up on to the sofa, and went right out through the open window. A second later, she was in the flowerbed in the front garden.

It had rained the night before, and the flowerbed was muddy and damp. As Daisy stood up, she realised that her blue dress was a bit stained and soggy.

"Never mind," she thought. "I have to keep going. I'll be all right once I've found a lovely new home."

Daisy had never been out on her own before, but she had been out with Laura dozens and dozens of times. She knew the way to Laura's friend Katie's house. She knew the way to the shops. And she knew the way to the park.

So Daisy picked up her case and her umbrella and began making her way down the garden. *Squelch, squelch, squelch, splotch* went her smart shoes in the mud. Her lacy white socks were soon soaked through, and she began to feel cold, but she made herself keep going.

By the time Daisy reached the pavement, it was nearly midday. She was exhausted. It is one thing to be pushed somewhere in a buggy, but quite another to have to walk there

on your own little legs. No wonder
the poor doll was tired! But Daisy
knew she had a long way to go, and
she wanted to get to the park before
nightfall, so she didn't stop.

As Daisy started her journey
down the pavement, the wind
began to blow and the sky grew
grey. Moments later, big heavy
raindrops plopped down on to
Daisy. She struggled to put up her
little blue umbrella, but it was so
tiny that the big drops of rain
simply splashed over the edge and
into her face. Soon her clothes and
her hair were soaked. In fact,
Daisy's whole self, right through to
her insides, was drenched and cold.

She was shivering terribly and felt faint.

"It's no use," Daisy said to herself. "I'll have to stop and rest, just for a bit. There are some leaves under those big trees … they'll be soft to lie on … I'll just rest for a little while … just a little while…" Wearily, Daisy collapsed on to the small pile of leaves. Her button eyes closed, and she fell fast asleep. All the while, the rain kept falling, and the wind kept blowing, colder and colder.

Hours later, Daisy woke with a start. The rain had stopped, but darkness surrounded the dainty doll. When she tried to move, she found she couldn't. She was trapped in a great heap of cold, wet leaves. In the tree above her, an owl hooted eerily and flapped its wings. The sound made the poor doll even more frightened. She was alone in a strange place, with no one to help her.

"Oh, what will happen to me now?" Daisy thought, trembling with cold and fear. Remembering Laura's soft, warm bed — and Laura's soft, warm arms around her — she began to cry.

"Why did I ever run away?" she sobbed. "How I wish I were back home, safe with Laura!"

As she lay there in the leaves,

weeping and wishing, Daisy suddenly heard something — a sound she
knew well. It was a bark, an excited,
happy bark, and it sounded so sweet
to Daisy.

"Max!" cried Daisy. "Max!
Help!" But she needn't have
bothered calling. Max knew just
where she was, and he was galloping

towards her. A moment later, she heard the familiar snuffle and felt Max's cold, wet nose nudging its way through the leaves. Then, ever so gently, Max grabbed hold of Daisy with his mouth and pulled her out.

"Oh, Max, you found Daisy!" cried Laura, running towards them. "Look, Mum!" she called. "Here she is! Oh, I can't believe it! Max found Daisy!"

When Laura took her and held her tight, Daisy felt happier than she ever had before.

"Let's have a look," said Laura's Mum, crouching down. "Hmm ... I think after a wash in some warm, soapy water and a little work with a needle and thread, Daisy should look as beautiful as ever."

"It doesn't matter what she *looks* like, Mum," said Laura. "The important thing is that she's back — and Max found her! You're a very clever dog, Max! You're a very clever dog indeed!"

As Laura reached down to give Max a pat on the head, Daisy looked down at him, too. Max was the only one who noticed that at that moment, Daisy's smile grew just a little wider, and one of her shiny button eyes winked. It was a wink that said, "I think you're clever too — friend!"

The Toy Train

IN THE NURSERY CLASS, there were lots of toys for children to play with. The little ones came every day for two hours in the morning and two hours in the afternoon. They did painting — and painted their faces as well as their pictures. They did modelling — and had to be stopped from eating half the clay. They did dancing — and sometimes kicked each other only half by mistake. They did singing — and sometimes you could recognise the tune!

In the afternoon, the children had a quiet time, when the teacher read them a story. They had a mug of juice or milk and some fruit, and some of them had a little sleep afterwards as well. Then it was time to play with the toys. And this time frightened some of the toys very much indeed.

"It isn't that they mean to be rough," said the ragdoll, one evening

after the children had gone home. "That little boy with the curly hair wanted to play doctors, and he decided to chop my leg off! It was lucky the teacher noticed in time!"

The other toys shuddered at this dreadful story.

"It was the same for me," said the rocking horse, shaking her silky mane. "If only the teacher hadn't read a story about zebras to those silly children, they would never have tried to paint purple stripes on me!"

"Just think yourself lucky you don't have wheels," grumbled the truck. "I can't remember the last time I had a full set of four wheels. If one of them is found, another is lost,

and I know that one of them is
under the toy cupboard, where it
will *never* be found. And don't talk
to me about my suspension! It's no
fun driving on your axles, I can tell
you. No fun at all."

"You're right there," agreed the
tractor, "and it's no fun being driven
into walls and doors and people's
legs either. And when a child bursts
into tears, it's never their fault, you
notice. Everyone complains that
there are sharp bits on the toys. They
say we're dangerous and should be
… I can hardly say it … thrown
away. I wouldn't have sharp bits if I
hadn't been bashed into a wall over
and over again!"

Now it happened about this
time that a kind aunty gave the
nursery class a brand new train for
the children to play with. It had a
shiny red funnel and bright blue
paintwork. Its wheels were black,
and its carriages were yellow. It
even still had its own cardboard
box!

The train had overheard the
toys' complaints. "That kind of thing
won't happen to me," it said to itself.
"When they see how shiny and new
I am, the children will be really
careful with me."

The next day, the train was
taken down from its shelf and given
to a little girl to play with. She

pushed it along quite happily for a while, but then she decided it needed some goods in its carriages. She put some modelling clay in the first one. She poured some paint in the second one. In the third carriage, she put half a sandwich left over from her lunch (and she had to squidge it a bit to make it fit). Then she had a wonderful time making the train crash into the long-suffering tractor.

By the time the children had put their coats on to go home, the train did not look like a new toy any more. Its paint was scratched and its funnel was bent. At least one of the teachers cleaned out its carriages and pushed the funnel back into shape before she went home.

That night, the toys grumbled as usual, and this time the train knew exactly what they were talking about.

"I'm not going to stay here with this kind of treatment," it said. "I'm off!" And to the amazement of the other toys, the train whizzed along the shelf and zoomed out of the top of the window, which happened to be open just far enough.

Crash! The train landed with a bump on the grass below, but all its carriages were still connected, so it felt ready for an adventure. The moon and stars were shining, as it set off to find a new home.

All that night, the little train whizzed along. At first it was travelling along pavements, but soon it came into the real countryside, where there were only roads with grass beside them. The little train soon found that it was not safe to chuff along on the roads. The puffing vehicle was too small for cars and trucks to see. One van almost squashed it, and another threw water from a puddle all over it. After that, the little train whizzed into a gateway and set off across a field.

It is not easy for trains to travel through tall grass and flowers, but as the sun rose, the little train felt quite cheerful. At least it was not about to be bashed or stuffed with stale sandwiches! All it needed to do was to find a new place to live, where it would be treated with some respect.

As luck would have it, the little train soon puffed into the garden of a large house. It was quite astonished to see another train whizzing towards it, travelling on a track laid all the way round the garden. The other train did not seem to want to stop to talk but zoomed past, blowing its whistle. The little train at once hopped on to the tracks and set off after it.

How much easier it was to travel on tracks! The little train enjoyed itself as it chuffed along. It was just giving a little *toot! toot!* as it went round a bend, when a large hand reached down and picked it up.

"Whatever is this?" asked a deep voice. It was the man who owned the house. He was a model-train collector, amazed to see a strange train chuffing round his tracks. "One of my friends must have put it here as a surprise," he said to himself. "Hmmm, it's not in very good condition. I must do some work on this one."

The train could hardly believe its luck. It soon found itself in the collector's workshop, where its scratches were painted and its funnel was made properly straight again.

By the time the man had finished, the train looked as good as new

— better than new, in fact, because it had been given a special polish that made it glisten and gleam.

Proudly, the man placed the train in a special cabinet, with a light above it so that everyone one could see how beautiful it looked. He wrote a little label and put it beside the train.

"I've really fallen on my wheels here," thought the train. "There could be no better place for a toy train to live."

It was true that the train never had to worry about being scratched and bashed. The man had so many different trains that he did not often take the little train from its cabinet.

Day after day, the little train sat there, looking perfect. There was not a speck of dust on its carriages or a smudge on its paintwork. It looked wonderful — and it *felt* very unhappy.

Isn't that train ever satisfied? you will ask. Sometimes it takes all of us a long time to find out what we really need. As it sat on its special shelf, the little train began to understand what all toys learn in the end: toys are meant to be played with, and they are not happy without children to love them — yes, and bash them and scratch them and squidge sandwiches into them sometimes as well.

It was several months before the little train had a chance to escape. Then, one evening, the collector took it into the garden for a whiz around the tracks. At the bottom of the garden, behind some bushes, the little train whizzed right off those tracks and off into the countryside.

It would be too much to expect that the little train found its way back to the nursery where it began, but it did find the house of a little girl and boy who were just delighted to have a new toy to play with. I would like to be able to tell you that they looked after the little train and were careful with it, but that wouldn't be true. They bashed it, they scratched it and they squidged not only sandwiches but several doughnuts and half a chocolate sponge cake into its carriages as well. Yes, they really loved their beautiful train.

And the little train? It has the kind of smile on his face that only a very bashed, scratched and squidged train can have. And, you know, it is as happy as a train can be.

The Lonely Panda

PAMELA PANDA belonged to a little boy called Jack. He played with her a lot when he was small, but now that he was a much bigger boy, he preferred his trucks and his little kitchen and his farm.

Toys expect that kind of thing. They know that children grow up and pass on to other kinds of amusements. It is a little bit sad, but very often the old toys are able to play together (when human beings are not looking, of course), so they have a happy life. Later, if they are lucky, they may be given to another little boy or girl, who will love and care for them just as well as the first one did.

Pamela Panda was a beautiful fluffy black and white bear. She had been given to Jack when he was a baby, and he loved to chew her black ears and lay his little head on her white tummy. Several times during those early years, Pamela had got dirty and messy, but she was a very *washable* bear, so when Jack's Mum had given her a twirl in the washing machine, she came out looking like new.

The unfortunate thing was that Pamela was such a favourite with Jack in the early days that the other toys didn't get much of a chance to play with the little boy.

"It's not fair," grumbled the

twin teddy bears. "He plays with that panda all the time, and she's no better than we are."

"She thinks she's superior to the rest of us," said the toy train. "You can tell by the way she points her nose in the air. I don't think she's very friendly."

In fact, Pamela Panda pointed her nose just the way it had been made back in China, and the toys knew that really, but they were upset that they were hardly ever chosen as playthings, so they pretended not to like her.

As time went on, the toys forgot that they really didn't know anything about Pamela. The stories

they had made up about her being cold and stand-offish were told over and over again, until everyone simply assumed that they were true. So none of the other toys talked to the panda at all.

Pamela was hurt by the other toys' attitude, but she didn't mind too much while Jack was her best friend. And perhaps she didn't try quite as hard as she might have done to be friendly, knowing that she always had Jack to play with.

"You see, we were right," the twin teddies would say. "She *is* unfriendly, just as we said. Well, if that's the way she wants it…"

Very gradually, Jack grew up.

Soon he was crawling around the room and pulling himself up on the furniture. He did still play with Pamela, but he didn't chew her ears or stroke her tummy any more. No, now he picked her up and whirled her round his head by the arm, before throwing her as far as he could across the room.

"Ouch!" Pamela Panda was glad of her soft fur to cushion her landing. She really preferred *not* to be thrown around like that, but it was better than not being played with at all.

Very soon, Jack took his first wobbly steps. Pamela watched with pride, convinced that she had helped him to grow so big and strong. She would have liked to have shared her pride with the other toys, but when she turned to them, they shrugged their shoulders and looked away.

As soon as Jack was toddling about the room, he lost interest in Pamela. Oh, sometimes he jumped up and down on her, and for a little while he still liked to have her in his bed at night, but more and more now she was simply left on the shelf. Poor Pamela felt very lonely. Perhaps now the other toys would be more friendly.

But during the day, the dolls and bears talked to each other, chattering so hard that there was no room for an outsider to make herself heard.

At night, the other toys cuddled up together, and the twin teddy bears had their own little cushion, where they slept next to each other. Poor Pamela didn't know whether the days or the nights were worse. She felt sad *all* the time.

About this time, Jack started to be very interested in books. He would sit with his Mum, turning the thick cardboard pages and looking at all the colourful pictures.

"Look, darling," his Mum would say, pointing to a picture of a truck, "that's just like your truck. And there

are some red boots, just like yours.
What else can you see on this
page?"

Jack would point to a picture
of a teddy bear and a train and try to
say the words.

"And look here," his Mum
would say. "Here's a picture of a
panda. Do you think it's a friend of
Pamela's?"

But Jack was bored now and
slipped off her lap to play with his
farm animals.

Jack's Mum put the book down
on a table, and as soon as her back
was turned, Pamela slipped across
and took a look at it. Yes, there was a
picture of a panda, and it looked just

like her! It had black ears and a white tummy, and it looked so friendly and cuddly. Pamela gave a big sigh. Why couldn't she have a twin like the teddy bears? It would be so lovely to have a friend to play with, especially a friend who was just like her!

Then Pamela had an idea. She had to wait until no one was around. Then she climbed up on to Jack's little stool and stood up. If she stood on the very tips of her paws, she could just reach to jump on to the dressing table, where Jack's Mum had put a large mirror.

Pamela raised her eyes slowly to the glass. There was another panda, just a pretty as she was, and it was smiling right at her!

"Hello!" said Pamela.

"Hello!" said the other panda.

Soon Pamela found that she could have lovely chats with the new panda.

At the back of her mind, of course, she knew that she was talking to her own reflection, but

she wanted so much to have a friend of her own that most of the time she didn't think about that.

The other toys simply didn't understand what she was doing.

"Just look at her," said the toy train. "She's so vain and stuck up she only ever wants to talk to herself. She's too good for us — at least, that's what *she* thinks!"

Things might have gone on in this unhappy way if Jack's cousin Joshua had not come to stay. Joshua was a year or so older than Jack and he was a *terror*!

Only two hours after Joshua's arrival, the toys were trembling in their shoes. He had stamped on the toy train. He had pulled the arms off the parachuting doll. He had made a little hole in the toy duck to see what his stuffing was made of. But worse was to follow.

That afternoon, Jack and his cousin went outside looking for adventures. They took with them some of the toys from Jack's room as part of the expedition team.

"We might want some of them to go first into dangerous places, to make sure it is safe," said Joshua wisely.

The toys shuddered as they were pulled along in the trolley that usually held Jack's bricks.

"What do you think they are

going to do with us?" whispered the twin teddy bears.

"Sshhh!" said the toy duck. "I've suffered enough already. I want them to forget I'm here."

Soon the boys reached the ditch at the end of the garden.

"We're not allowed to go across," said Jack. "Mum won't let me."

"No, but we could throw these toys across," said Joshua, "and see which ones can reach the other side."

Jack wasn't sure at first, but he was quite keen to show off his throwing, which, as we know, was pretty good.

"All right," he said. "I'll go first!"
And he picked up one of the twin
teddy bears and threw it as far as he
could, right over to the other side of
the ditch.

The boys had a lovely time,
before long both the bears, and the
toy duck, and Pamela Panda were
lying in a heap on the other side of
the ditch. Then Jack and Joshua
went off to have their lunch and
forgot all about the rest of their
expedition.

Out in the cold field, the toys
were moaning and groaning.

"We'll never be found here on
the ploughed earth. It's just the same
colour as our fur," said one of the

teddy bears. "We'll have to stay here all summer. Then the farmer will plough us up and that will be the end of us!"

But Pamela Panda was busy wriggling and jiggling on the bottom of the pile.

"Just let me get to the top," she puffed.

"Oh, that's typical," said the toy duck. "Why should you be on top of the pile, that's what I'd like to know?"

"Because," said Pamela, "I'm black and white. I'm the one that Jack's Mum will be able to see from far away when she comes to look for us this afternoon."

The toys were silent for a moment. What Pamela had said was certainly very sensible. They let her wriggle her way to the very top.

"Now," said Pamela, "it may be a long time before we are rescued, so I suggest we sing some songs and tell jokes. It will keep our spirits up."

The toys could hardly believe their ears. Was this the stuck-up panda who preferred her own company to theirs?

That afternoon, as they all lay together in the field, the toys learnt a lot more about Pamela, and she learnt a lot more about *them*. But one of the teddy bears was still not sure.

"What I don't understand," he said, "is why you spend so much time looking in the mirror. You're a fine looking panda, I know, but even so, it looks rather vain."

Then Pamela explained that she had been so lonely, she had talked to her own reflection sometimes, pretending it was another panda.

The toys were silent for a moment. Then they all spoke at once and from their hearts.

"We're sorry," they said. "Let's all be friends now, shall we?"

"Oh yes," agreed Pamela. "And here comes Jack's Mum. We'll soon be safe and sound."

The Singing Bear

ONCE UPON A TIME, there was a teddy bear with a beautiful voice. When you shook him gently, he made a deep, growling sound. When you poked his tummy, he made a friendly, humming sound. And when you patted him firmly on the back, he said quite distinctly, "Hello! I'm Bernard Bear!"

As you can imagine, Bernard Bear was a great favourite in the nursery. All the children loved to play with him, and best of all they liked to make him talk. In fact, if you shook, poked and patted Bernard in the right way, you could have quite a long conversation with him. It was lovely for the little ones.

But Bernard Bear was not content with the sounds he could make. He thought that he could do better. One day, a little girl brought a musical box to the nursery. When you opened the lid, a little dancer

inside twirled round and round, and music played. It was quite soft and tinkling, but everyone could hear that the musical box played "Twinkle, twinkle, little star."

Bernard Bear was most impressed by the box. "If a silly thing like that can sing a tune, then surely a clever bear like me can do it," he said to himself. "It's time I started to practise."

Bernard Bear was determined to sing at all costs. He took a deep breath and opened his mouth. "Grrrrr," he said. "Grrrrr. Grrrrr. Grrrrr."

Bernard Bear tried again. This time he took an even deeper breath.

"Hmmmm," he said. "Hmmmm. Hmmmm. Hmmmm."

This was no good at all. Bernard Bear took an enormous breath, so that he was full of air. He opened his mouth as wide as it would go. He clenched his paws and… "Hello!" he said. "I'm Bernard Bear!"

Poor Bernard! It didn't matter what he did or how hard he tried, he could only make the noises he had always been able to make. Of course, he could talk to other toys, but that wasn't what he wanted. He wanted to be able to sing to the children who played with him.

"You should think yourself

lucky," said the toy train. "I can only whistle to humans. At least you can say a few words."

"Yes," agreed the toy duck. "If

you squeeze me very hard, I sometimes squeak, but even that doesn't work if I've been left in the bath for a long time."

But Bernard just wasn't satisfied. "It's all very well," he said, "being content with what I can do already, but I'm an ambitious bear. I want to impress everyone I meet. I want people to say, 'Oh, yes, we know Bernard Bear. Isn't he amazing?' That's what I want."

"You should be careful, Bernard," said the toy train. "You might make matters worse, not better, with all your practising."

Nothing anyone could say would dissuade Bernard from

pursuing his singing career. He listened hard when the children in the nursery had their singsong each afternoon. He had soon learned the words and the tunes — but he still couldn't sing the songs! So Bernard listened even harder to what the teacher had to say.

"Now children," she said. "Lift up your heads and take deep breaths. I'm going to open the window so that you can breathe in all that lovely fresh air. Then we'll sing this song as loudly as we can. Let's see if we can't wake up Bernard Bear over there and make him growl!"

"I'm not asleep, actually,"

muttered Bernard, but it was nice to be mentioned, all the same.

When the children had gone home that night, Bernard thought about what the teacher had said. Fresh air! That was the answer. He must fill himself up with more fresh air.

Bernard hopped over to the window and nudged it open with his paw. It slid up quite easily.

"Now, the way to get most fresh air will be to sit on the windowsill," said Bernard to himself. "Let's see. If I put one leg this side and the other leg this side, I can *just* balance."

Bernard Bear sat on the

windowsill and took a deep breath.
Then he took another deep breath.
Then he took a third deep breath …
it was a breath too many. With a
wobble and a wiggle, Bernard Bear
overbalanced and fell right out of
the window.

Plop! Bernard fell heavily on to a flowerbed below the window. His face was muddy. His paws were muddy. His tummy was muddy. You would hardly have recognised him as the fine bear who sat on the nursery shelf.

Next day was sunny, so the teacher took the children outside. It wasn't very long before one little boy found Bernard in the flower-bed.

The teacher took charge at once. "Let me have a look at that bear," she said. "Oh dear, he's been outside all night, I think. I'll have to take him home with me and clean him up."

That night, the teacher did her best with Bernard Bear. She rubbed him and she scrubbed him, until his fur was as clean as ever. Then she brushed him with a lovely soft brush and put him near the radiator to dry.

"Phew!" said Bernard to himself. He felt that he had had a lucky escape.

Next day, looking as bright and bonny as usual, Bernard was taken back to the nursery. Two little girls immediately claimed him to join in their game.

"What do you say today, Bernard?" they asked, shaking him gently.

Bernard said nothing.

"Don't you want to talk to us, Bernard?" asked the little girls, poking the bear's tummy.

Bernard said nothing.

"Tell us who you are!" laughed the little girls, patting Bernard on the back.

But Bernard said not a word.

Whether it was the rubbing and the scrubbing, on the bump into the flowerbed, or simply being outside one whole night, there was no doubt about it. Bernard had lost his voice.

"If only I hadn't tried to sing," moaned Bernard to himself. "I had a lovely voice before, but now I'm just as silent as most other teddy bears. I should have been happy with who I was."

Bernard certainly had learnt his lesson, and a few days later, when one of the children gave him a little shake, he found himself making a tiny noise.

"Grrrrr," he said. "Grrrr. Grrrr."

Perhaps Bernard will get his voice back after all. I hope so, don't you?

The Beep Beep Car

ONCE UPON A TIME, there was a teddy bear who had a car. Yes, he had a real car, in which he zoomed about all over the place. He visited his friends and took them for outings. He did shopping for toys who were too old or busy to go into town themselves. He even delivered cards and presents when it was Christmas time.

In fact, he was a very useful bear to know, and everything would have been fine if only he hadn't been so noisy. Well, it wasn't really the bear who was noisy. It was the car. Beep! Beep! Beep! Beep! It was terribly loud.

The teddy bear's friends never

had to look out of their windows to see if he was coming. Oh no. From miles away you could hear his car beeping. There was plenty of time to have a cup of tea, and read the newspaper, and put your coat and hat on before he arrived at your door!

Some of the teddy's friends tried to tackle him on the rather tricky subject.

"Your car is a wonderful machine," began the ragdoll, working her way towards the important part. "But tell me, does it have to make such a loud beeping noise?"

"Oh yes," said the teddy bear. "That's half the fun. Why, no one would know I was coming if it wasn't for that beeping noise."

"That's very true," agreed the ragdoll, "but you know, there are times when we don't really want to know you are coming. I mean, the other week, for example, the poor old train jumped right off his tracks because you beeped as he was going round a corner. He did terrible damage to his axles, and he has only

started to get over the shock just recently."

"Well, I'm sorry to hear that," said the teddy bear, "but really that train is going to have to pull himself together. Whoever heard of a car that didn't go beep! beep! sometimes? I certainly never did."

"It's not so much that it goes beep! beep!" the doll went on. "It's that it does it so loudly."

"Well, you know," replied the teddy bear, "there's not much point in a beeper you can't hear. That's what they're for, you see."

The doll couldn't think of anything else to say after that. The teddy bear had a point in a way, but she still felt that his car was much, much louder than any other car she had ever heard (and that included the racing cars in their shiny box, and everyone knows what a loud noise they make!)

One day, the teddy bear decided to take some of his friends to the seaside. They packed up some sandwiches and their swimming costumes and set off along the road to the coast.

When they reached the seaside, the teddy bear parked his car as near to the sea as he could. Further along the beach, a policeman doll waved his arms at the toys.

"You see how everyone likes my car?" said the proud teddy.

The toys went down on to the beach and were soon having so much fun that not one of them noticed a little row of waves splashing on either side of them.

After some games and some sandwiches, the toys all had a snooze in the sunshine.

It was the ragdoll who woke up first, and she looked happily around.

"How lovely it is to be sitting on a little island like this," she said to herself. "Wait a minute … an island? This wasn't an island when we arrived!"

The waves were lapping on every side of the toys and the little

car. Anxiously, the ragdoll woke the other toys.

"It's too deep to wade," said the teddy bear. "How are we ever going to let anyone know that we are here? There's no one in sight at all. We could drown before help comes!"

But the ragdoll smiled. "I think your car's very loud beep is about to be useful," she said.

In two minutes, the toys were all inside the car, beeping the horn for all they were worth. At least, the teddy bear beeped, and the other toys kept their hands or their paws over their ears. Beep! Beep!

It was not long before the toys

were rescued by the waving policeman in a boat. "I did try to warn you," he said.

"What about my car?" asked the teddy bear, as they were rowed away. "I do hope the waves won't dampen its beep."

"We should be so lucky!" laughed the toys under their breath, now that they were safe and sound.

The Teddy, Bears Picnic

ONE DAY, Mrs Carolinus, who taught the smallest children at the nursery school, clapped her hands for attention and used her loudest voice.

"Children!" she called. "I have a special announcement to make, and you will each have a letter to take home to your parents. Next week we shall have a special outing to raise money for the new playground. It will be a Teddy Bears' Picnic! You

can each bring your bears — but only one teddy bear each, please — and something nice to eat or drink. I'm sure we shall all have a lovely day."

The children were very excited at the news.

"My teddy bear's name is Honey," said Lauren. "He'll love coming to a picnic."

"My teddy bear has beautiful white fur and a special stripey jacket all of his own," said Carla. "He's been all over the place. I took him with me when we went overseas on holiday last year, so a little picnic won't be so exciting for *him*."

"I don't know *which* of my

teddy bears to bring," said Annabelle grandly. "I've got *ten*, you know. Some of them are really too beautiful to bring outside, and others are *huge*, so I really couldn't carry them. I'll have to think about what to do."

One little girl listened to her friends talking and kept very quiet. Sally only had one teddy bear, but she loved him more than all her other toys. He was very old and rather threadbare. Two of his paws had worn out and been replaced by Sally's Mum, so he now had two blue paws and two pink paws. What Sally loved best about Rory (for that was her bear's name) was that he had been given to her by her Granny,

who had moved two years earlier to live far away on the other side of the world. Sally missed her Granny terribly, but when she cuddled her old bear, she knew that her Granny loved her and was thinking about her.

"The other girls will laugh at Rory," said Sally to herself. "Poor old bear. He can't help being worn and mended."

But when Sally took the letter home to her Mum that afternoon, Mum couldn't see a problem.

"Rory is a little bit shabby because he has been loved so much," she said. "Would you want to swap him for a brand new bear?"

"Oh no," said Sally. "Never!"

The day of the picnic soon arrived. The weather was bright and sunny — just right for a lovely day out of doors. Sally's Mum had made some chocolate buns and some cheese rolls for her to take to share with the other children. She wrapped them up and put them in Sally's school bag.

"There doesn't seem to be much room in here, Sally," said her mother as she tried to tuck the food away. "Just a minute. What's this? You've put Rory in the bottom of your bag! He won't be able to see anything in there! Poor old bear!"

Sally hung her head. "I'm sorry,"

she said. "I was just afraid that the others would laugh at him, because he's not fluffy and new, you know."

"The only important thing is what *you* think about your teddy bear," said Mum. "If you don't laugh at him, it doesn't matter one bit what other people think. What would Granny say if she could see Rory hidden away?"

Sally knew that her mother was right. She put her bag over one shoulder and tucked Rory under the other arm.

"Come along, Rory," she said. "We've got a picnic to go to!"

Mum took Sally and Rory to the place where everyone was

meeting for the picnic. It was on the outskirts of a beautiful wood. Mrs Carolinus had a list of all the children's names, and she ticked them off as they arrived.

Soon there were twenty children, all clutching their teddy bears, waiting to set off. Two other teachers had come along to help Mrs Carolinus.

"Now, before we go," called Mrs Carolinus, "I want you all to listen very carefully to what I have to say." (She was using her loudest voice again.) "It is very easy to get lost in a wood like this one," she went on, "so you must all keep up with the person in front. No dawdling! And no one, whatever happens, must stray off the path. Do you all understand?"

"Yes, we understand!" called the children.

"Then we are ready to begin," said Mrs Carolinus. "Quick march, everyone!"

The teachers and the children set off. To begin with they walked side by side, but soon the path through the trees became narrower,

so they had to walk in single file. In places, bushes and brambles almost covered the path, so the teachers had to hold them out of the way as the children went past. Mrs Carolinus called out all the time to make sure that no one got lost.

"Are you there, Annabelle? All right, Sally? Keep up, Carla!"

The children had to concentrate so hard on following the person in front that there was no time to look at other bears or compare them. Sally began to feel better.

"This *is* an adventure, isn't it, Rory?" she whispered.

When they had been walking

for about half an hour, and were deep in the forest, Mrs Carolinus called out very loudly.

"Everybody stop!"

Unfortunately, some children stopped more quickly than others, so there was quite a bit of confusion and one or two dropped teddy bears. Soon everyone had picked themselves up and dusted themselves down. Mrs Carolinus called out again.

"Now we can't stop here for our picnic because there are too many bushes and brambles," she said. "We will have to walk a little way from the path to find a clearing where we can all sit down together."

"But I thought she said we mustn't leave the path?" whispered Carla.

She knows best," said Annabelle. "After all, she *is* a teacher."

One by one, the children and teachers followed Mrs Carolinus, until they found a lovely clearing where they could spread out a cloth and all the delicious things they had brought to eat.

What a feast it was! And Sally didn't have to worry about anyone thinking Rory was old and shabby because everyone was much too interested in having something to eat to notice *what* her bear looked like.

At last, the children and the teachers could not eat any more. In fact, there was not very much *left* to eat! Walking in the woods had certainly given everyone an appetite. Mrs Carolinus called out again.

"We shouldn't start walking again immediately after our picnic," she said. "We must give our tummies a chance to settle. Let's sing some songs instead. Now, who knows any songs about teddy bears?"

The children had a lovely time. They sang the song about teddy bears bouncing on the bed and the one about the three bears. And, of course, they sang the song about the teddy bears' picnic — twice!

"Now, collect up your things," said Mrs Carolinus, "and please be very careful not leave anything behind. We must leave these beautiful woods as free of litter as we found them. And whatever you do, *don't* leave your teddy bears behind!"

"As if I'd leave you, Rory," whispered Sally, as they all formed a line once more.

But for the first time, Mrs Carolinus seemed a little bit uncertain. She looked around and had a few words with the other teachers.

The children saw them shaking their heads and looking a little worried. Finally, Mrs Carolinus spoke up.

"It's this way!" she called. But her voice didn't sound quite as sure as it usually did.

The children and the teachers walked for five minutes before Mrs Carolinus told everyone to stop and not to move.

"We should have reached the path by now," she said, "so I think we are slightly off course. Follow me, and we'll soon be back on track."

The children followed their teacher, whispering excitedly to each other. "Do you think we're lost?" they asked. "What are we going to do if we can't find our way home?"

Five minutes later, Mrs Carolinus called a halt again.

"This way isn't quite right either," she said. "The other teachers and I are just going to have a little talk about the best way home. Don't wander off!"

The children sat down on a nearby grassy bank. Now, for the first time, they looked at each other's bears.

"Goodness me, Sally," said Annabelle, "what a very old bear you've got there. It must be nearly an antique!"

"Yes, he's very valuable," said Sally, which wasn't strictly true, but it made her feel better, and

Annabelle didn't say anything else about Rory.

After ten minutes, Carla, who had been keeping an eye on the little group of teachers, leaned forward and whispered to the others. "You know," she said, "I think we really *are* lost. I just heard Mrs Carolinus say that the best thing would be to stay where we are and wait for someone to come to look for us."

"But it will get dark!" said Annabelle. "I don't want to be in this creepy wood when it's dark!"

"Well, I don't think anyone knows the way home," said Carla, "so we don't have much choice really."

Just then, Sally heard a little whispering sound in her ear. It was Rory, trying as hard as he could to attract her attention.

"What is it, Rory?" Sally asked her old bear.

"I couldn't help overhearing what you were saying," said Rory, "and I'd like to suggest that you give

the *bears* a chance to find the way home."

"Whatever do you mean?" asked Sally in surprise.

"Well," said Rory quietly, so that the other children couldn't hear, "I don't expect anyone has thought of this, but bears are used to woods and forests. That's the kind of place they come from, after all. We notice things that human beings never think about, such as whether a tree might have bark for a bear to scratch, or where there might be a hollow tree trunk to shelter in when it is cold and wet."

"So what?" hissed Sally.

"So I think I can tell the

difference between one tree and the next much better than that teacher of yours," explained Rory. "But you'll have to pretend it was you who noticed, because she'll never believe me."

Sally looked long and hard at her bear. "Why don't the other bears know the way as well?" she asked slowly.

"Perhaps some of them do," said Rory. "I haven't had a chance to ask them. But, you know, most of the bears here are rather *young*. They probably haven't learnt very much about woodcraft yet."

Sally was convinced. She and Rory whispered together for a few more minutes. Then the little girl picked up her bear and made her way to where Mrs Carolinus was sitting, looking rather anxious and upset.

"Excuse me," said Sally, politely, "but I think we are really very near the path, you know. I'm quite sure we passed that tree with the silvery bark on our way here."

Mrs Carolinus looked very doubtful, but she was ready to clutch at any straw. She sent one of the other teachers over to the silvery tree to have a look. Two minutes later, the teacher was waving excitedly. It *was* the path! They were not lost after all!

It was a tired but happy group of teachers and children who found their way to the meeting place half an hour later. The parents had begun to look at their watches, wondering what had happened to the party.

"Ah," said Mrs Carolinus quickly, "there were so many good opportunities for nature study in the woods, I'm afraid we rather lost track of time."

"We certainly lost track of something," whispered Rory, with a giggle.

That night, when Mum tucked Sally up in her bed, she asked what the other children had thought of Rory.

"They said he was old and shabby," said Sally, "but you know, I don't mind at all. There's a lot to be said for being old."

Mum couldn't help but smile at Sally's serious little face. "I'll tell Granny you said that!" she laughed, turning out the light.

The Every-Year Dolls

DIANA PICKED UP her last Christmas present. She had opened all the rest, and they had been full of wonderful surprises. But this present was different.

"I don't really need to open this," she said. "After all, we know exactly what's going to be inside it."

"Well, not *exactly*," her mother protested. "I do know what you mean, darling, but it is very, very kind of Granny to make a special present for you each year, especially now that her eyesight is not so good. And her fingers are not as nimble as they were, you know."

Diana did know, and she tried hard to be grateful, but it really was very hard. She couldn't help sighing as she undid the brightly coloured paper.

It had all started when Diana was three. Granny had made her a beautiful little doll, with a yellow satin skirt and a bright blue top. She had black silky hair and little red boots, and the smiliest, jolliest face you could imagine. Diana had really loved that little doll, the tiniest of the dolls she had. It was partly because she was so small and partly because Granny had made her specially — just for her.

Of course, both Diana and her mother had told Granny how very pleased she was with her present.

Perhaps they had said so just one time too many, for the next year, Granny made another doll. It was exactly the same as the first doll, except that this time it had a pink skirt and a white top and little blue boots. Oh, and its hair was golden.

Diana quite liked having sister dolls. They looked just right sitting either side of the table in her dolls' house. She told Granny how pleased she was — and she meant it. Granny smiled and admired the dolls' house.

But the next year, when Diana was five, Granny made her *another* doll. It was exactly the same as the first two, but with different coloured clothes again and red hair this time.

"For the dolls' house," wrote Granny on the card that came with the carefully wrapped parcel.

As the years went by, Granny became more and more frail. She could not travel to see her grand-daughter any more, but she still made dolls. Each Christmas a similar parcel arrived, and each time there was a little doll inside, almost, but not exactly, like the very first one.

Diana still wrote a nice letter each year, thanking her Granny. She knew that it took the old lady longer and longer each time to make the doll, but each one was as perfect as the one before. Diana was rather old now to play with dolls, and the last thing she wanted for Christmas was *another* of the every-year dolls, as she called them, but she didn't want to hurt the old lady's feelings if she could help it.

The very last doll didn't arrive at Christmas. It was the twelfth doll, and Diana was fourteen. Granny was very ill that winter. At the end of November, a telephone call came to say that Granny had passed away peacefully in her own home. A few weeks after Christmas, Diana's mother travelled to Granny's house to sort out her things and make preparations for its sale. She found the twelfth doll, almost complete, in Granny's workbasket. Only its eyes, nose and mouth had not yet been added.

Diana's mother brought her the last doll. "I know Granny would have wanted you to have it, darling," she said.

It was many years since Diana had seen Granny. She felt a little bit sad because her mother was sad, but she did not really miss the old lady. And she certainly did not miss the every-year dolls. She put the last doll, with the others, in the box that contained some of the toys she had played with as a child, and soon forgot all about them.

Almost twenty years passed. Diana went to college and worked hard. She became a doctor and worked even harder. Then she got married and had a little girl of her own — and she worked harder still.

In all that time, Diana had not thought about her box of toys, but one day, watching her baby daughter playing with a new plastic doll, she suddenly thought of the box tucked away in the attic. When the baby was in bed, she found the box and brought it downstairs.

As she opened the box, Diana felt the years slip away. One by one, she took out the little dolls, but now she looked at them with different eyes. She noticed for the first time how beautifully they were made. The stitches were tiny. The fabrics were soft and in lovely colours. Best of all were the tiny faces, each with its own laughing expression. For the first time in years, Diana thought of her Granny and all the patience and love that had gone into each tiny doll. Tears came to her eyes.

It was almost Christmas again, and Diana could not bear to put the dolls away again. Her own little girl was much too small to play with them — they were so perfect and fragile.

Diana picked up the dolls one by one and put them side by side along the mantelpiece. Their outstretched arms touched each other, as though the twelve little dolls were holding hands. They looked lovely.

As Diana stood and looked at the dolls, her husband came into the room. Glancing at the mantelpiece he said, "Oh, you've started putting the Christmas decorations up. How lovely!"

Diana smiled. It was only a few weeks before Christmas. Now she knew exactly what to do with the little dolls.

That evening, Diana carefully sewed the dolls together, so that one little hand clasped the next. Last of all, she found some embroidery thread and gently put two eyes, a little nose, and a mouth on the last little doll. She took a long time over it, for she wanted it to be just as fine as the other dolls. Then she pinned up the string of dolls above the mantelpiece, where they looked as bright and colourful as any Christmas decoration.

As Diana's baby grew older, she noticed that the dolls were put in the same place each Christmas.

"They're so pretty," she said. "Where did they come from?"

So Diana told her the story of the twelve little dolls.

"And will we have them *every* year?" asked the little girl.

"Of course," said Diana. "They are every-year dolls — and always will be."

The Surprise Box

ONCE THERE WAS an annoying little boy who had a habit of guessing what was in the presents he was given each year for his birthday. You can imagine what it was like. A kindly aunt would come to visit, holding a present with bright wrapping paper and a ribbon tied in a great big bow.

"Happy birthday, Robert," she would say. "I hope you like this."

Robert would take the present, shake it, prod it, pass it from hand to

hand and, without undoing it, say, "Oh, it feels like socks. Thank you very much, Aunty Joy."

"Well, yes, it is," Aunty Joy would say, looking disappointed. "Aren't you going to open them?"

"All right," Robert would reply, "but it's not so much fun when it's not a surprise."

Now this was hardly fair. No one forced Robert to guess what was in his parcels. It was just a pity he seemed to guess so well. In fact, Robert was very lucky, after a while, that his friends and relations *gave* him presents. It wasn't much fun seeing him open them, after all.

One year, Robert's Uncle Paul

decided to teach him a lesson. He came to visit on Robert's birthday as usual and put a large box on the table in front of his only nephew.

Robert picked up the box. He shook it. He turned it round. He prodded it. He lifted it up and down. He even sniffed at it! He had to confess that he hadn't a clue what was inside.

"Well, open it," said Uncle Paul.

Robert felt rather more interested in this present than in some of the others he had been given. He undid the ribbon and carefully took off the paper. Inside … was another parcel!

"Now you can guess, I expect,"

said Uncle Paul. Once again, Robert went through his shaking, prodding, sniffing routine. He still couldn't tell what was in the parcel.

"So open it," smiled his uncle.

Paul undid the next ribbon. He took off another layer of wrapping paper to find ... yes, you've guessed, yet *another* colourful present inside.

"Can't you guess yet?" teased Uncle Paul.

Robert scowled. He did everything he could think of to the parcel and wished he had an X-ray machine. He still couldn't work out what was inside.

"Open it!" laughed Uncle Paul.

Once again, Robert undid the wrapping paper — only to find another colourful layer inside.

"I don't think there's anything inside here," said Robert. "It's just layer after layer of paper."

"Oh no, it isn't!" said Uncle Paul. "There's quite definitely a present in there, but I'm amazed that you can't work out what it is. You're usually so clever."

That made Robert even more cross. He tore off more and more and more paper, until at last he came to a brightly painted wooden box.

"*Now* what do you think it is?" asked his uncle.

Robert shook the box. There

was no sound. He tapped it. It didn't sound hollow or full, just ordinary. He sniffed it. It didn't smell of anything except wood.

"Well?" asked Uncle Paul. "What is it?"

Robert had to smile. "I don't have a clue," he said. "It's the first present I haven't been able to guess for *ages*." Then he grinned more broadly.

"I suppose," he said, "there is one thing I can say that it definitely *is* … it's a surprise!"

And it was! Turn the page to find out what Robert saw when he opened the box!

Woah! Rocking Horse

What do you do with a rocking horse who is wild? One who bucks and gallops and generally acts as though he is out on the open plains, free to do as he likes? The rocking horse at the Tiny Tots Playgroup was just like that.

In fact, it wasn't really that the rocking horse was nasty and vicious. He didn't mean to send so many little children tumbling from his back when he put on a spurt of speed or kicked up his legs. It was just that the children, very often, were excited to be sitting on the beautiful rocking horse. They grabbed his mane in their plump little hands and kicked their strong little legs into his sides. Well, any horse will get excited as well, if he is treated like that. Sometimes the children shrieked with joy as the horse began to move, and that just made him worse. What with the kicking and the tugging and the shrieking, the rocking horse would leap into action. He would begin to move faster and faster, rearing and rocking higher and higher, until the children screamed with fright

instead of excitement and several of them, as I said before, fell right off on to the carpet.

Luckily, no one was hurt by the wild rocking horse, but most of the children were badly frightened, and they certainly didn't want to sit on the rocking horse again. They didn't understand that if *they* were gentle with the rocking horse, he would be gentle with them.

It was not surprising that the rocking horse soon had a very bad reputation. "Don't go near that horse," the playgroup leader would tell the children. "It's not safe at all."

With no one to ride him, the rocking horse became very sad.

Unfortunately, when a brave child did jump on his back, the rocking horse was so surprised and pleased that he kicked up his heels more than ever. It really was a vicious circle.

Then, one day, a new little girl came to the playgroup. She had been

in hospital for a long time and was still very frail and pale. Although she was nearly four, she couldn't walk very well, and had to be lifted in and out of her chair to sit on the floor at story-time or join the other children singing nursery rhymes.

The little girl did not seem to be interested in anything very much. She had spent so much time by herself that she had forgotten how to play with other children. In any case, she felt so ill and tired a lot of the time that nothing interested her much.

But when the little girl, whose name was Tina, had been at the playgroup for a couple of days, she noticed the rocking horse in the corner.

"I want to ride on *that*," she said. It was the longest sentence that anyone had heard her say.

"I don't think so, Tina," said the playgroup leader. "That horse isn't very safe, and you are not very strong yet. Wait until you are feeling better."

But Tina didn't want to wait. She felt as if she had spent all her life waiting — waiting to go into hospital, waiting for an operation, waiting to feel better, waiting to run around like other children of her age.

Day after day, the little girl

made the same request, and at last
the playgroup leader agreed. After
all, nothing else seemed to interest
Tina

The playgroup leader cleared a
big space on the floor. She put down
a lot of cushions, in case of
accidents, and stood nearby to catch
the little girl when she fell — as she
was sure she would.

But when Tina sat on the
horse's back, she didn't pull his
mane or kick her feet. She sat quietly
and held the reins, feeling the horse
beginning to move, ever so slowly.

The playgroup leader was
amazed. Gradually, she began to relax
and moved away from the horse, for

he was behaving beautifully. No pony ever trotted so gently with a little girl on his back. The horse went slowly, slowly for half an hour, getting to know his rider, until Tina became tired and asked to be lifted down.

After that, Tina rode the big rocking horse every day. And very, very gradually, the horse began to speed up.

As Tina grew stronger, she was able to sit up straighter and hold the reins more tightly. Her eyes began to sparkle and a faint pink colour came to her cheeks. She began to take an interest in other things that were happening at the playgroup, too.

Every day she grew happier and healthier.

On the last day of term, Tina's parents came to take her home from playgroup. They were very pleased with the way she had been

improving, but they had never seen her ride the rocking horse, and they did not know why her eyes were brighter and her smiles were broader.

The playgroup leader greeted Tina's parents as they came into the big room. In the corner, a little girl was riding the rocking horse, higher and higher, and faster and faster, her hair flying out behind her as she rode.

"Ah," sighed Tina's mother, "how I hope the day will come when our little girl can do that. It has been such a struggle for her, though she *is* so much better now."

The teacher laughed. "That *is*

your little girl," she said "And she's as wild as the rocking horse — I'm very happy to say!"

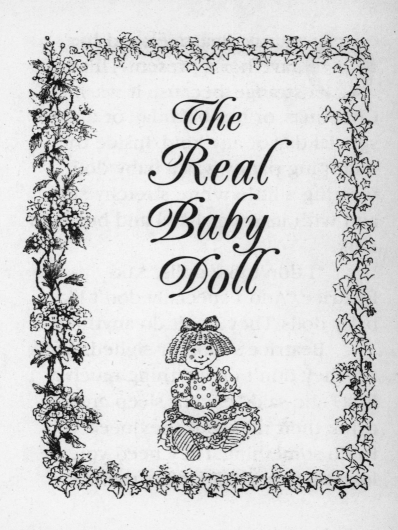

The
Real
Baby
Doll

ONE DAY, Beatrice's mother gave her a present. This was strange, because it wasn't Christmas, or her birthday, or a special day of any kind. Inside the wrapping paper was a baby doll, wearing a little white stretchy suit and with its own shawl and bottle of milk.

"I don't like dolls," said Beatrice. "And I specially don't like baby dolls. They don't do anything."

Beatrice's mother sighed. "Well, no, they don't do anything much at first," she said, "except sleep and drink their milk, but they need you to do something. They need you to love them and look after them. I think you could do that, Bea, couldn't you?"

"Why should I?" asked Beatrice. "I like toys that move or play tunes or light up or something. Not like this silly doll."

The little girl's mother tried again. "The reason I thought you might like a baby doll to look after," she said, "is that I'm going to be having a baby soon — a little sister for you, Bea — and I thought it would be fun if we could both look after our babies together."

But Beatrice looked at her Mum with a big scowl on her face. "You can take this doll back," she said, "and you can take your baby back, too. We're quite happy as we are, aren't we? We don't need one of those silly babies here. Don't let's talk about it any more. Promise?"

"I can't take either of the babies back, Bea," said her mother gently. "Perhaps you'll change your mind in a little while."

But Beatrice continued to show no interest at all in the baby doll. Her mother showed her how to wash it and feed it and cuddle it. But Bea was always impatient to get back to her other toys. She hid the doll in a cupboard, but somehow her mother always found it and brought it out again.

A few weeks later, Beatrice's

father came into her room late one night. "Aunty Julia has come to look after you tonight, Bea," he said, "because I'm going with Mummy to get our new baby. Isn't it exciting?"

"Well, I hope you're not going to bring it back here," said Beatrice. "I told Mummy we don't need it."

But in the morning, Daddy came back and carried Beatrice into the sitting room. Mummy was propped up on the sofa, and in her arms she held a little pink and white bundle.

"Come and see our baby, Bea," she said, and she looked rather anxiously at her little girl.

Beatrice came forward and put

out her hand. She touched the baby's soft little hand and cried out in amazement. "But she's warm! She's not like a doll at all!"

And the baby, hearing her sister's voice, closed her little fingers around Beatrice's thumb.

"Oh, Mum," breathed Beatrice, "I've got such a good idea. You can have my baby doll, and I'll have this one. She's much, much nicer." And she bent down to kiss the little head.

"Let's share her," said her mother. "This little one belongs to all of us."

Della Duck's Adventure

WHEN AMY was a baby, her big brother gave her a yellow duck to play with in her bath. Amy loved playing with it from the start. She tried to drown it every night, but the little duck always came bobbing up to the surface again, as large as life.

A few weeks later, Amy tried to get rid of the duck in another way.

Over and over again, she threw it as far as she could with her chubby little arms. She got so good at throwing that the duck often hit the bathroom wall and bounced back again, sometimes falling with a *plop!* right back into the bath. Night after night, Amy's mother, or her father, or her big brother patiently picked up the duck and put it back in the water.

As Amy got bigger, the duck had lots more attacks to suffer. One summer's day, Amy threw it right out of the bathroom window, which was open a tiny bit at the top.

"That child should play basket-ball," said her father, admiring the

little girl's aim. As the family lived on
the sixth floor of a block of flats,
Amy's big brother had to hurry
down several flights of stairs to find
the little duck out in the car park.
After that, Amy's parents kept the
bathroom window shut *all* the time.

I'm afraid Amy's next game
with the duck was even worse. She
(this is quite embarrassing) tried to
flush him down the lavatory! Amy
was not very pleased when the little
duck came bobbing up again, and
Amy's mother was not very pleased
either at having to fish out the duck
and take it away for a thorough
cleaning and disinfecting before Amy
could have it back again.

Not surprisingly, Amy didn't want to play with the duck for a while, but as the years went by, she found that the little yellow bird was extremely useful in lots of different games. It made a wonderful target. As Amy grew up, the duck had bean bags, pingpong balls, arrows and even pretend grenades thrown at it.

Later on, Amy used the duck for lots of different experiments. She took it to school and catapulted it

across the playground and into a nearby field to show how levers work. She took it to summer camp and let it float right out into the middle of a lake to practise her life-saving skills. She took it to the park and perched it on the edge of a pond to see how real ducks would

react to it (they either ignored it or pecked it).

After all that, you might have thought that the duck would be rather scratched and bashed, but it actually looked as fresh and bright as the day it was made. With its yellow body and orange beak, the duck looked as good as new.

During all those years, the duck was given many names. Amy's father called it "The Indestructible Duck". Amy's big brother called it "The Unthinkable Unsinkable", but Amy one day named her duck after one of her teachers, who had a voice rather like a quack! After that, it was always Della Duck.

You might think that Della
Duck had already had enough adventures to last a liftetime, but Amy had
not finished with her yet. In her last
year at school, Amy took part in a
balloon race. You probably know all
about them. Hundreds of people
write their names and addresses on
labels hanging from balloons. Then
the balloons are released and float
far away. When the balloons finally
come to rest, sometimes months
later, anyone who finds them can
post off the label, saying where the
balloon was found. The person
whose balloon is found to have
travelled the farthest is the winner.

It would be silly, really, to

attach anything else to the balloon, because it would weigh the balloon down and stop it travelling so far, but one or two members of Amy's class started adding little things to their balloons, and the craze spread. Some people tied on a tiny teddy bear or a photograph of themselves. I don't suppose I need to tell you what Amy decided to tie on to her balloon.

At last the day came when all the balloons were released. Up they went, pink, purple, blue, yellow and green — and one of them had a very brave little duck attached to it!

After a few days, some of the labels from the balloons began to arrive. They had been found many miles away. After a few weeks, even more labels had been returned, and some of them came from hundreds of miles away. But as the weeks turned into months, there was no news of Amy's balloon, or of her old friend Della Duck.

"The balloon might have landed in the middle of a forest or in a desert," said Amy's brother. "No one will ever find it there. Or it might have come down over the sea."

"Well, that would be all right," retorted Amy. "We all know that Della can float. In fact, that duck is impossible to sink."

"True enough," said her brother,

"but that doesn't mean that anyone would *find* her. There's an awful lot of ocean out there, after all."

Even several months after the balloon competition, labels were still arriving, even though the finishing date had passed. A very few balloons had travelled right across the sea and reached other countries. Some of the balloon-senders began writing to the people who had returned the labels, for they felt as if they were special penfriends.

But there was no news of Della. Finally, Amy had to admit that it was very unlikely that the duck would now be found. It could be anywhere in the world by now.

"You're right," Amy told her big brother. "That duck could have fallen in a quarry or a jungle. I just wish I knew where Della was, that's all. I'd just like to *know*."

"Well, you played with that duck longer than I ever thought you would," laughed her brother. "It's the most successful present I've ever given you."

On Amy's next birthday, her brother gave her a tiny box. "I thought we should mark a sad occasion," he smiled. "I hope you like them." Inside the box was a pair of tiny earrings — shaped like ducks!

"Now I'll never forget Della," laughed Amy, "wherever she is!"

It was not long before Amy left school. She had been wondering for a long time what kind of job she might like to do. Somehow, thinking about Della and where she might be in the world made Amy feel that she too would like to travel — not attached to a balloon, perhaps! Amy was lucky to find a job quite soon that was just what she wanted. She worked for a travel agency, and after a year or so began to travel all over the world, seeing many of the places that she had only dreamed of before.

Amy loved her job, especially as she sometimes was able to stay a few extra days in the places she visited, so that she could have a little holiday of her own. It was when she was lying on a beautiful, sunny beach on the island of Hawaii that the most extraordinary thing happened.

Amy was feeling hot and went down to the edge of the sea for a

cooling swim. But as she came to the edge of the water, Amy kicked something in the sand. She thought it was a shell or a pebble and almost didn't bother to look down, but something made her kneel down on the warm sand and take a look. A little orange beak was poking out of the sand!

"Della!" cried Amy, brushing away the rest of the sand. It certainly was a little yellow duck, and it *looked* just like Della, but whether it really was that famous duck I couldn't say.

Amy wrapped the duck up carefully and sent it to her brother, who now had a little boy of his own. "For Toby," she wrote on the label, "hoping Della has even more adventures with you."

Well, she did, you know, but that is quite another story and for another time…

The Smiling Star

EVERY NIGHT, when Jenny was tucked up in bed, her mother said the same thing:

"Sweet dreams, darling. Shall we sing our bedtime song?"

And Jenny and her mummy would sing, ever so softly:

Star light, star bright,
First star I see tonight,
I wish I may, I wish I might,
Have the wish I wish tonight.

Then Jenny's mother would give her a kiss and put out the light. With the words of the song still ringing in her head, Jenny would crawl down to the foot of her bed and peep through the curtains. Sometimes it was cloudy, and there were no stars to be seen. In the summertime, it was often too light to see the stars. But when she looked

out and saw a dark, clear sky, with little twinkling lights so high up and so far away, Jenny breathed a sigh of happiness. Then she shut her eyes and wished for the thing she wanted more than anything else in the world.

When she was a very tiny girl, Jenny wished for toys, or a visit to the playground, or even something really nice to eat for her supper next day. Sometimes her wishes came true, and sometimes they didn't, but

that wasn't really important because they were only little wishes. Now Jenny had a really big wish, and it mattered very much indeed whether it came true or not.

It had all started a few months before. Jenny's mummy and daddy started to have really big arguments. Jenny sometimes found her mummy in tears, although she brushed them quickly away when she saw her little girl. Daddy seemed unhappy too. He hugged Jenny and played with her as much as ever, but at breakfast and supper time, both he and Mummy were unusually quiet, with their eyes on their plates.

Jenny knew that something

was badly wrong, and at first she thought it was somehow her fault. She tried to be extra good and helpful. She tried not to talk more than she had to, and she just crept away when the horrid arguments started.

But one day, Jenny's mummy noticed how quiet and good she was being, and asked her what was the matter! Jenny explained that she was trying to make everything all right again, so that they could be a happy family.

Jenny's mummy hugged the little girl and sat her on her lap. She explained very gently that sometimes mummies and daddies don't get along so very well together. She reassured Jenny that it wasn't her fault in any way at all, and she promised that Jenny would not hear any more arguments.

After that, things were a little better. Jenny's mummy and daddy didn't argue in front of her, but Jenny was pretty sure that they still did it in private, because both of them had sad faces and were very quiet when they were together.

Then, one day, Jenny's daddy took her to the park to feed the ducks. As he and Jenny sat together on a bench, he explained that there were going to be some changes.

"I'm going to live in another

house in future," he said. "And you and Mummy will move to a little house somewhere very nice. I'll see you ever so often, and we'll have lots of fun together. I love you lots and lots and lots. Everything will be fine."

But Jenny couldn't help bursting into tears.

"I don't want you to go," she sobbed. "Please stay with us."

Jenny's daddy held her close and stroked her hair.

"I have to go, honey," he said. "Mummy and I both think it's the right thing to do, and in the end, we'll all be much happier. You and Mummy will have lovely times together, and when I come to see you, *we'll* have lovely times, too."

Jenny was still very upset, but she tried to be brave. Next day, Daddy didn't come home from work at his usual time.

"Daddy has gone to live in his new house," said Mummy. "And I have found us a lovely little cottage in the countryside. I know that you will like it, Jenny. There are cows and sheep and horses in the fields all around. And you will be able to have a rabbit of your own, if you like, just as you have always wanted."

That night, Jenny and her mummy sang their special song as usual:

Star light, star bright,
First star I see tonight,
I wish I may, I wish I might,
Have the wish I wish tonight.

For the first time, after her mother had closed the door, Jenny scuttled down to the end of the bed and peered at the sky as if her life depended on it. Thank goodness! There was one little star, twinkling in the sky.

"I wish my daddy would come home again," whispered Jenny, squeezing her eyes shut. "I wish it with all my heart."

All that week, Jenny made the same wish. Then, on Saturday, some men came with a truck and loaded all the furniture from the house into it.

"Come on, darling," said Jenny's mummy. "We're going to move into our new house today. I know that you will love it. Have you got all your toys?"

Jenny clutched her favourite teddy bear and followed mummy to the car. She looked back at the house where she had been so

happy, and tears rolled down her little cheeks.

"It will be all right, honey," said her mummy, hugging her. "I promise it will. New things are often upsetting, but everything will be fine."

"Everyone keeps saying that," sobbed Jenny, "but it isn't fine. It isn't all right."

Mummy started the car and looked as if she might cry too.

"It will be," she said. "Much sooner than you think, it will be."

On the way to the new house, Jenny and Mummy stopped for a snack at a little restaurant. Jenny knew that this was a special treat, and usually she would have loved it. But today the ice cream tasted horrible, and she couldn't finish her milkshake.

"I don't feel very well," she said, pushing her food away.

Mummy felt her forehead and looked at her carefully.

"Then we must hurry up to reach our new home," she said. "You can settle down and rest until you feel better. It's not much farther, and there's a surprise waiting for you there."

The countryside certainly was pretty, as they drove along the winding road to the little village where their new house was to be found. Even Jenny could not help noticing the pretty little lambs jumping in one field. There was nothing like that in the suburbs where she had lived before.

At last Mummy stopped the car and pointed to a little pink cottage with a thatched roof.

"That's where we're going to live," she said. "Isn't it nice?"

Jenny had to agree that the cottage did look pretty. It was the kind of place she had always wanted to live, only she had wanted to live there with her mummy *and* her daddy.

Mummy showed Jenny all over the cottage, including the little bedroom under the eaves that the little girl would have for her very own. Jenny peered out of the window and noticed that there would be a very good view of the stars in the night sky. So *that* would be all right.

"I'm not going to stop wishing just because we've moved here," she said to herself.

"Now," said Mummy, "come outside, and I'll show you your special surprise. Shut your eyes and take my hand."

Jenny followed her mother out into the garden. She felt the sun on her face and could smell lovely scents from the flowers as she passed them.

"Now," said Mummy, "open your eyes!"

Jenny opened them and blinked in the bright sunshine. Then she looked down at a little piece of grass with a fence around it.

"Oh!" cried Jenny. "Is he really for me?"

"Yes," smiled Mummy, for the

first time that day. "He's all yours. What are you going to call him, darling?"

Jenny looked at the dear little white rabbit sitting on the grass.

"I'm going to call him Snuffles," she said, "because of the way he's wiggling his nose. Oh, he's just what I always wanted. Look at his lovely ears and his little pink nose! I'm going to take ever such good care of him."

"I know you will, sweetheart," said Mummy. "I've bought you a little book about how to do it."

"Yes," said Jenny. "I want him to stay with me always. I don't want *him* to go away."

Jenny's mummy said nothing, as she went back into the cottage to start unpacking.

That night, Jenny slept for the first time in her new bedroom. She had her old bed, of course, and all her familiar things about her, but still it felt strange.

Mummy came in as usual to say goodnight and sing the Starlight Song. Jenny could hardly wait for her to close the door. Creeping out of her bed, she went over to the little window and looked out.

How much bigger and nearer the stars seemed than in the town, where the streetlights were so bright! Jenny gasped as she looked

up at the velvety night sky. There
was the moon, and there were
hundreds and hundreds of little stars
twinkling in the darkness.

Jenny looked at one star in
particular and made her wish. I'm
sure you can easily guess what it
was. The star seemed to twinkle as if
it was answering her.

Then Jenny crept back into her
bed and closed her eyes. It had been
a long, tiring day after all.

Almost at once, the little girl heard a tapping on the window. *Tap tap! Tap tap!* it went. Jenny didn't feel at all frightened. She just wondered very much what the strange sound was.

There was nothing else to do. The little girl got out of her bed once more and went to the window. There had not yet been time to put up new curtains, so she could see at once what was making the tapping sound, and she couldn't have been more surprised if Father Christmas himself had been sitting on the windowsill outside.

It was a star! Yes, a shiny yellow star with little arms and legs and a big beaming smile. Jenny rubbed her eyes. She knew that stars didn't come knocking on people's windows in the middle of the night.

But the little star knocked again. *Tap tap! Tap tap!* Almost without thinking, Jenny lifted the catch and opened the window.

"Good evening," said the star. "You wished?"

"Sorry?" said Jenny.

"*I'm* sorry," said the star. "Didn't that make sense? You wished, so I came. How can I help you this fine starry night?"

"I'm afraid I don't understand," said Jenny. "I've wished lots and lots of times, but I've never seen a star before."

"It's the interference," said the star. "It's a terrible problem for us. In towns there is so much light that children's messages often don't get through. But your wish was beautifully clear tonight. You'd like your daddy to come home, I believe. Now, you will get cold if you keep the

window open like this. I'll just hop inside and then we can talk properly. How would that be?"

Jenny was all too happy to invite the star into her bedroom. She hopped back into bed, and the star sat comfortably on the bedside table with his legs crossed. He was still smiling.

"Now," he said, "what has happened to your daddy?"

Then Jenny explained all about the arguments and the new houses. She even told the star about Snuffles.

"I see," said the star. "Poor you. Will you be able to see your daddy sometimes? Or has he gone to live a long way away?"

"Oh no," said Jenny. "He's very near, and he's coming to see me every weekend."

"Well, that is very good," said the star. "Now this kind of thing happens quite a lot, you know, and the best thing to do is always to wait a little while and see how things go. What I would like you to do is to spend a few weeks getting used to your new home. You can have fun with your daddy and with your mummy, and I will come to see you every night to make sure you are all right. Then we will have another little talk and see how things are going."

The star did sound as if he

knew what he was talking about, so Jenny agreed to do just what he suggested.

The next few weeks passed more quickly than she could have imagined. She met lots of new friends at her playgroup, and she explored the garden and the countryside beyond. There was a nice man who kept bees in the next cottage, and he had a little girl too, so Jenny and her new neighbour often played together.

At the weekends, Daddy came to see Jenny. They had lots of fun and talked about all kinds of things. In fact, they seemed to have a nicer time than they ever had before.

Daddy had so often been busy with work from the office or doing jobs around the house at the weekends.

Mummy seemed to be enjoying putting the new house in order too. She made pretty curtains for the windows and a beautiful rabbit hutch for Snuffles, who was as cosy as could be with his straw and his food and water.

All this time, Jenny carried on making the same wish each night. She didn't even have to think about it any more. The words came into her mind as soon as she looked out of her window and saw the stars.

"I wish my daddy could come and live with us," she said.

Each night, the smiling star came to visit Jenny. Sometimes he didn't stay very long, but at other times they sat and talked long into the night. When they had finished, Jenny would open the window, and the little star would whizz right up into the night sky.

The star talked about all kinds of things. He told Jenny about the North Pole and how cold it was there. He explained that it was cold like that in space, too, but that stars didn't mind. He described the many countries that he had seen on his travels and talked about the planets as if they were old friends. He told Jenny about some of the other children he visited, too.

Then one night, he said, "It's time we talked about your first wish, Jenny. I have some questions to ask you."

"All right," said the little girl. "What are they?"

"Would you say that your

mummy is happier now?" asked the smiling star.

Jenny thought about hearing her mummy singing as she made Snuffles' rabbit hutch. She remembered the fun they had had together, choosing new things for the house and deciding what to do in the big, rambling garden.

"Yes," she said. "I think she is much happier now."

"And is your daddy happier?" asked the smiling star.

Jenny thought about the way that daddy didn't have those creases in his forehead any more. She thought about all the lovely times she had had with him each weekend. He looked sort of younger somehow.

"Yes," said the little girl. "I think he *is* happier."

"And now for the really important question," said the star. "Are *you* happier, Jenny?"

Jenny thought hard. There were no more arguments. At mealtimes now, she chattered merrily. There were no more awkward silences. And it was lovely living in the country. And then there was Snuffles. She felt so grown up looking after him all by herself.

"Yes," she said. "I do feel happier too."

The smiling star smiled even

more broadly. "Then do you think you should make a different wish each night?" he asked. "Why don't you think about it?" Jenny was rather quiet the next day.

"Are you all right, darling?" asked her mother.

"Yes, I am all right," said Jenny, almost as if she was surprised to find that she was. "We're both all right, aren't we?"

"Yes, we are," smiled Mummy, giving her a hug.

That weekend Jenny asked Daddy if he was all right.

"I'm very all right," laughed Daddy. "Race you to the swings!"

When Mummy came to say

goodnight that evening, she sang the special song with Jenny.

Star light, star bright,
First star I see tonight,
I wish I may, I wish I might,
Have the wish I wish tonight.

And Jenny looked out of the window and made a new wish.

"I wish we can all be happy, wherever we live," she said. And you know, her wish came true.

The Ship of Dreams

ONCE THERE WAS a mighty ship, with sails of silver and ropes, which are called sheets on a ship, of gold. It had a poop deck and a quarter deck and all the other decks a ship should have. It had portholes and a rudder and masts. But the strange thing is that it didn't have a crew. No, the ship sailed all by itself.

Which ocean did this ship sail upon? Did it cross the great Pacific Ocean or drift across the warm waters of the Indian Ocean? Or did it brave the great storms of the Southern Ocean? No, it sailed none of these great seas. It sailed the skies. For it was a ship of dreams.

If you go sailing on the ship of dreams, you will visit strange lands and meet people who look almost familiar. You might zoom through the skies or plunge to the bottom of the seas. You could ride on the back of a tiger or take tea with a flea. The ship of dreams can sail anywhere, but it always comes back to port in the morning.

Once there was a little boy who wanted more than anything else to go sailing on the ship of dreams. But in the morning, he could never remember if he had dreamed or not. At school, his friends would talk about the wonderful dreams they had had, but poor Peter could

never remember a single one. After a while, he felt so left out that I'm afraid he began to invent dreams that he had not had at all.

"Last night," he would boast, "I dreamed I was riding on a camel. It had a bridle of gold and reins of silver. We travelled over the desert for miles and miles, until we came to a beautiful palace. Everyone bowed down when I went into it. I was the Prince of the whole country, and I owned the palace and everything in it."

"Wow!" said the other children. "I wish we had dreams like that."

"Oh, that was nothing," said Peter. "The night before that I dreamed I was diving in the ocean and saw a wreck on the sea bed. I swam down to it and found a casket full of jewels. They glinted and glittered in the blue water. But just as I was swimming down to reach them, a huge shark came charging towards me. It opened its mouth and…"

"Yes, yes?" cried the children.

"…and I woke up," said Peter.

Peter soon found that everyone wanted to hear about his fabulous dreams. He began to make them more and more elaborate and extraordinary. One day, as he was telling the children about a trip through a forest, where wolves were howling, his teacher happened to overhear him.

"With an imagination like that, Peter," she said, "you should be a writer. You have kept your friends spellbound for an hour."

And when Peter grew up, he did become a writer, a very famous writer. His stories were read and loved the world over.

When Peter was an old, old man, a journalist came to see him to write a story about his life.

"How lucky you were to have such rich dreams to draw on in your early years," he said.

"No," said Peter. "In fact, I did not have dreams at all, but that was lucky too, in a way. I had to use my imagination to make up strange tales for myself, because as far as I know, I never dreamed."

"But everyone dreams!" the young man protested. "It must just be that you don't remember."

"I don't know," said Peter. "I only know that as far as I'm concerned, the ship of dreams has never stopped for me, and I would give all the stories I have ever written and all the money I have ever made for one trip upon that wonderful ship."

The journalist left the old man sitting looking wistfully out to sea. He wished that it was in his power to give the great author what he wished for.

But that very night, Peter dreamed of a fabulous ship, with sails of silver and sheets of gold. It was the ship of dreams, and he ran on board as nimbly as he would have done when he was a boy. The places Peter visited that night and the people he met will remain a secret

for ever, for his first and last great dream was one from which he did not awake. He has sailed on for ever, into the setting sun.

Princess Dreamy

ONCE UPON A TIME, there was a Princess who spent her life dreaming. Even in the middle of the day, you could find her sitting by herself, fast asleep or simply gazing into space. The King and Queen were rather worried about this, so they called all the most respected doctors in the land to give their considered opinions.

"It is a grave disease," said one doctor, "called *somnomulous revex*. Only very, very intelligent and sensitive people can catch it. Indeed, almost all the cases that have been recorded have been among royalty. Why, the King of Pandango suffered for years."

"And is there a cure?" asked the King, anxiously.

"Alas, Your Majesty, there are some afflictions that nobility must bear," said the first doctor. "I can prescribe some medicines that will ensure your daughter's good health, but I cannot take away her dreamy condition."

The second doctor stepped boldly forward.

"I must disagree with my learned colleague," he said. "The Princess's condition is not caused by an illness at all. She has clearly been bewitched. We shall need to find some powerful magic to counteract the spell that has been cast upon

her. I could recommend someone, if Your Majesty wishes. I'm afraid that if an antidote to the spell is not found, your daughter will stay like this for ever."

"That's dreadful," said the King. "Yes, please, do give me the name of a reliable … er … spellbinder."

But the third doctor was already bustling forward.

"With all respect to my most esteemed colleagues," she said, "what I have heard so far has been complete nonsense from first to last. It is quite plain to me that someone has put a sleeping draught into your daughter's food. You should inter-rogate all your servants and have every morsel of her food checked by a reliable taster. I have the names of several reputable practitioners here if Your Majesty wishes. I can vouch for each and every one of them personally. I think Your Majesty will find that after a few days, the Princess will be her old self again."

"By all means give me the name of a good taster," said the King, although he privately wondered how his daughter was going to be able to eat *anything* if a taster ate every morsel — there wouldn't be any untasted morsels left!

Now a fourth doctor pushed his way to the front.

"We have heard a number of

extraordinary opinions here today," he said, "and I don't doubt that my colleagues have all diagnosed your daughter in good faith, but they could not be more wrong. The Princess has quite obviously been hypnotised. It may have been a person who did it, or the Princess may have inadvertently hypnotised herself by listening too long to the ticking of a clock or the dripping of a tap."

"There are no dripping taps in *my* palace," put in the Queen, rather sharply. "But please do go on, doctor."

The fourth doctor blushed but continued.

"We shall need a very skilled

treatment to bring the Princess back to her old self," he said. "Luckily, I myself trained in Zurich under the great Professor Pamplemouse. I would be willing to undertake the cure at once, but of course I would need all these people to be cleared from the room." With a sweeping gesture of his arm, the doctor indicated all the other doctors and courtiers standing around the King and Queen.

The King looked at his wife a little desperately. Then he turned to the crowd.

"Naturally, the Queen and I are anxious to do whatever is necessary to cure our only child," he said. "We have heard many learned opinions today, and we must think carefully about what to do. I beg you to leave us now and allow us to think over what you have said. We will give our decision in the morning."

The doctors bowed and walked backwards out of the room. Some of them were clearly not used to this manoeuvre, for they fell over their gowns and had to be rescued by the courtiers standing by. It was a sight that would normally have made the King roar with laughter, but today he was much too worried about his daughter to smile.

Soon there was no one in the room but the King, the Queen, the

Princess and the little serving maid who looked after her. The Princess sat dreamily looking out of the castle window, paying no attention at all as the little maid combed her long, dark hair.

The King and Queen sat down together to discuss the opinions of the four doctors and decide what to do about their daughter.

"I don't know about *you*, my dear," said the King, "but I am well and truly confused. Can all these experts be right? Surely our darling girl cannot be so unfortunate as to be suffering from *somno*-some-thing, *and* an evil spell, *and* a sleeping draught, *and* hypnotism all at the same time? That would be dreadful."

"I agree with you," said the Queen. "All of the diagnoses sounded sensible at the time, but now I don't know what to think. I suppose we could try each of the cures in turn?"

"And put our daughter through

four lots of treatment?" asked the
King. "That would surely make her
worse than she is now. After all, it's
not that she is in pain, or even
unhappy. She just isn't exactly *with*
us most of the time."

"You are right, my dear, of
course," said the Queen. "Our
daughter's wellbeing must be our
first concern. But I am still uncertain
about what to do."

Just then, a little voice from the
corner of the room spoke up. It was
the serving maid.

"Excuse me, Your Majesties,"
she said timidly, "but I spend a great
deal of time with the Princess. Might
I just say something myself?"

"Of course you may," said the Queen kindly. "I know that you are very fond of your mistress and would not want any harm to come to her. What is your opinion of what we have heard today?"

"Well, Madam," said the little maid, curtseying deeply, "I have seven older sisters, and I have seen every one of them suffering from much the same illness as the Princess."

The King was a little shocked. "You mean it's not an illness that only royalty can suffer from?" he asked with a frown.

"I don't think so," said the little maid. "I think it is something that

almost anyone can suffer from. My sisters were just like this. They sat by themselves. They sighed and didn't hear people talking to them. They gazed out of the window all the time. But I am very happy to say that each one of them has now recovered."

"So what was this illness from which they all suffered?" demanded the King, although the Queen was beginning to look as though she understood, and a small smile played about her lips.

Before the little maid could answer, she turned to the King and said, "You know, I had forgotten, but I believe I suffered from much the same malady around the time I first met you, my dear."

The maid smiled too, for the Queen was blushing and looking very pretty.

"Well, you two seem to know what you're talking about," muttered the King, a little gruffly. "Suppose you let a chap who's still in the dark into the secret?"

The little maid curtseyed again. "To put it plainly, Your Majesty," she said. "I believe that the Princess is in love."

"In love?" cried the King. "Why, that's preposterous! She's much too young, and besides, who can she possibly have met that she could be in love with?"

"Don't be so silly, dear. She is two years older than I was when I married you," said the Queen briskly. "And if you remember, young Prince Beaumont was here only last month. He stopped by on his way to visit his aunt, the Grand Duchess."

At the mention of Prince Beaumont's name, the silent Princess turned first white and then pink, causing the Queen and the serving maid to look triumphantly at each other. The King groaned loudly.

"I see only too clearly that I shall have no say in this matter," he said, "although in truth I like young Beaumont well enough, and it could have been much, much worse. If she wants that young Princeling, and he feels the same, I won't stand in their way."

At that, the Princess ran across the room and threw her arms around her father. Having spent several secret afternoons with the

Prince, she knew only too well that he had the same feelings for her as she had for him. The King was astonished, but pleased. And the Queen immediately began to plan the biggest royal wedding that the world had ever seen.

As for the little serving maid, she became a Lady-in-Waiting of the First Rank, for when it comes to knowing what is the matter with ordinary mortals, common sense is often a great deal more useful than any amount of learning, even from Professor Pamplemouse in Zurich!

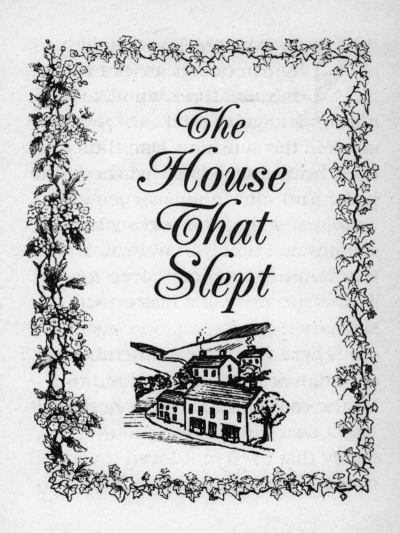

The House That Slept

NOW EVERYONE knows that human beings are not the only creatures who like to curl up and go to sleep. Cats love to sleep in the sunshine. Ducks tuck their heads under their wings on the pond. And some animals, such as tortoises, sleep for months and months at a time. But did you know that houses sometimes sleep too? This is the story of a house that slept.

There was once a little house at the edge of a wood. It had red tiles on the roof and a green front door. It was a dear little house, and the family that lived in it loved it very much.

There were six of them altogether. Mr and Mrs Ruggles had four children. That was a lot of people to squeeze into a very little house, but they were a happy family and got along very well. Mr Ruggles worked in the woodland, clearing fallen branches and felling trees when the time was right. He walked to his work each day and enjoyed it enormously. He felt that he was a lucky man to live where he wanted to live and work where he wanted to work.

Mrs Ruggles worked in the nearby town. She was a nurse, visiting people in their homes and making sure that they were taking care of themselves properly. She too enjoyed her work. She even enjoyed the journey into town each day, driving along the pretty, winding road through the beautiful countryside.

The children went to school in the town too, but they were always glad to come home to their little house next to the wood.

The family took care of each other, and they took care of the little house, too. Each year, Mr Ruggles climbed up on to the roof (while Mrs Ruggles stood below and called to him to be careful) and checked that none of the red tiles were loose or broken. And every other year, Mr

and Mrs Ruggles painted the front
door and the windows, to keep out
the rain and frost. As they grew
older, the children helped with the
painting, too, so that a job that once
took a whole week was finished in
two days.

The children grew up, as children do, and one by one they left home to study, or work, or find homes of their own.

Soon, only Mr and Mrs Ruggles were left. At first the house seemed very big without the children, but Mrs Ruggles said that they couldn't possibly go and live somewhere smaller because the children would need somewhere to sleep when they came home for visits. Mr Ruggles was secretly very relieved to hear his wife say this. He loved living so near the forest, and he loved the old house. It had so many happy memories.

But time passed, and first Mr

Ruggles and then Mrs Ruggles retired from their work. They still loved their home, so they decided not to move, although their children all thought that would be a good idea.

"It's so lonely out here," they said. "What if one of you became ill and needed a doctor?"

Mr and Mrs Ruggles laughed.

"We're not quite in our dotage yet, you know!" they said.

But it was harder now to look after the little house, even without having to worry about work as well. Now that there were only the two of them to do the painting, it took three weeks – much longer than before. And they had to call a man out from the nearby town to check the tiles, because Mrs Ruggles said that it just wasn't safe for her husband to climb on to the roof any more.

There were other problems, too. Although he still liked to live near the wood and watch as it changed through the seasons, Mr Ruggles was upset by the way his old work was now done by machines and lads who had no feeling for the beautiful trees.

"It's not the same," he said. "It breaks my heart to see them carting logs away as if they were sacks of coal. Those trees are living things.

They should be treated with respect."

Then, one very cold winter, snow lay so thickly around the little house that Mr and Mrs Ruggles were trapped for two weeks. They were no longer strong enough to clear the snow from the driveway, and they were worried about dangerous ice on the winding road into town.

The couple sat in their armchairs either side of the fire and looked at each other.

"We've had a wonderful time in this old house," said Mr Ruggles, "but it's time we moved into a little bungalow in town."

"Yes," said Mrs Ruggles. "I shall

be sad to leave here, but it will be a relief, too, in a way."

So Mr and Mrs Ruggles locked the green front door for the last time and followed the van containing their furniture and all their possessions along the winding road. They were very happy in their new home and soon hardly ever thought of the little house near the wood.

Meanwhile, a board was put up outside the house. "To Let," it said. "Contact Buttle and Bung, Estate Agents." Several people came to look at the house, but it was either too small, or too far from town, or too lonely, or too old-fashioned. After a few months, the estate agents' board fell down in a high wind, and no one bothered to put it up again. Standing by itself, next to the lovely woodland, the house fell fast asleep.

Of course, it didn't shut its eyes, for houses don't have eyes, but they have windows, and these gradually grew dull and dusty. The paint on the front door began to fade and peel. The red tiles, which Mr Ruggles had looked after so carefully, began to slip and slide, and some of them fell off altogether.

Then, of course, the rain began to trickle into the house. It dripped through the ceilings and made puddles on the floors.

But the house wasn't empty. Oh

no. All kinds of little creatures made
their home there. Spiders filled the
corners with cobwebs. Little ants
and beetles crept along the dusty
floorboards. Moths fluttered around
the windows. In the walls, little feet
could be heard scampering night
and day, as a group of mice moved in
and brought up their own families.
An owl perched on the guttering
some moonlit nights.

So the house slept on, and the
trees crept nearer to it, until their

branches touched the roof and pushed more of the tiles into the garden. Well, it wasn't a garden any more, really. The plants rampaged everywhere, and some of them reached right up to the bedroom windows. If you weren't looking carefully, you could walk right past the house and not know it was there. It was having a long, long sleep.

Then, one day, Mr and Mrs Ruggles' eldest son came back to visit the place where he had grown up. He brought his wife and their two young children with him.

"I'm so looking forward to seeing it," said the younger Mrs

Ruggles. "You've talked so much about it. I'm sure it was a perfect place for a child to live."

When he turned off the long, winding road from town, her husband couldn't believe his eyes. The trees and hedges along the drive had grown so much.

"It all looks so different," he said. "And, oh no, I don't believe it! The house has gone!"

"No," said his wife, for she had seen a chimney sticking up above the bushes. "It's still here, hidden behind all this greenery."

"It's a secret house," laughed the children. "Let's go and look inside! It's an adventure!"

It took ages to push aside the branches and wade through the grass to the front door. The lock had rotted away, so it was easy to swing the door back on its creaking hinges and step inside.

"Be careful," warned Mr Ruggles. "The floorboards may have rotted,

and it doesn't look as if the ceiling is too safe either."

The grown-ups and the children tiptoed through the rooms. The house was in a terrible state, but somehow it still felt like a happy place to be.

As the children ran out to explore the garden — which they called "the jungle" — their mother and father looked at each other and saw that they were both thinking the same thing.

Mrs Ruggles laughed. "It would be mad!" she said. "There's so much work to do on it!"

Mr Ruggles smiled too. "It would be stupid," he agreed.

His wife sighed. "It would be a wonderful place for the children to grow up," she said.

"We'd never find another house in such a beautiful spot," said her husband.

Soon they were both giggling like children.

"It's time we did something completely crazy again," said Mr Ruggles. "Let's go and explore the jungle."

Over the next few weeks, there was more activity around the house than there had been for the last ten years. Trees were cut down, and bushes were pruned. Soon it was possible to reach the front door without a struggle. But still the house slept.

Over the next few months, workmen hammered and sawed. Timbers were renewed and floorboards replaced. New red tiles were put on the roof, and the front door was mended and painted — green, of course. But still the house slept.

At last the day came when Mr and Mrs Ruggles and their two children moved in. Lights winked at the windows, and the house felt a warmth inside that had been missing for a long time. The house stretched and creaked for a moment — and woke up at last.

Wake Up, Muffin

CATS LOOK so comfortable when they are asleep. Somehow they always manage to find the warmest, cosiest spot in the whole house. And often it's the very spot where you most want to sit yourself!

But some cats seem to want to sleep most of the time, and that can be particularly annoying if what you'd really like to do is to play with them.

Helena had a cat called Muffin. The little girl loved him very much. She couldn't remember him when he was a kitten, because she was only a baby herself then, but even now, Muffin wasn't an old cat. He was only four, just like Helena.

But Helena was a lively little girl, and Muffin was a very sleepy cat. Very often, when Helena wanted Muffin to join in one of her games, he was fast asleep on the sofa.

"Wake up, Muffin!" Helena would call, bending close to one of the cat's furry little ears.

Muffin's ear would twitch, just a little bit.

"Wake up, Muffin!" Helena would shout, louder this time, bending a little closer.

Muffin's ear would twitch a little bit more. Helena would take a deep breath and lean forward until she was almost touching the soundly sleeping cat.

"Wake up, Muffin!" she would yell, so loudly that her mother could hear her from the kitchen.

And Muffin? He would open one lazy eye. He would twitch his whiskers and have a little stretch. And he would go right back to sleep again.

It was so annoying! Helena tried being extra specially nice to Muffin. She stroked his fur gently and tickled his fat tummy. She sang him little songs about mice and kittens. But nothing worked. Muffin would simply purr with pleasure and stay fast asleep.

One day, Helena badly wanted Muffin to play with her. She was tired of her dolls, who were nothing

like as warm and cuddly as her cat.
She put her doll in its pram and
tucked a quilt round it.

"You just go to sleep like a good
girl, Hettie-Marie," she said (for that
was the doll's name).

Helena searched everywhere for
Muffin. He wasn't on the sofa, which
was his favourite place. He wasn't
under the table or next to the
radiator. At last she found him fast
asleep (of course!) on the quilt of
her parents' bed.

As she looked down at the
sleeping cat, Helena had a brilliant
idea.

She bent down and gently put
her arms around Muffin. He wasn't

very heavy as she lifted him up and cuddled him next to her, and he didn't move a muscle. He was fast asleep as usual.

Helena carried Muffin into her bedroom. She took silly Hettie-Marie out of her toy pram and tucked Muffin in instead. He looked so sweet!

All day, Helena played with her new baby. And what a good baby he was! He didn't cry and he didn't try to climb out of his bed. He looked lovely wrapped up in a lacy shawl, and he looked absolutely gorgeous with a little blue bonnet on his head!

Best of all, when Helena lifted him out of his pram or his cradle and held him in her arms, he was warm and cuddly, not cold and hard like her dolls.

So now, if you visit Helena's house, you hardly ever hear a piercing shout of "Wake up, Muffin!" ringing through the place. In fact, you are much more likely to hear Helena complaining very quietly when her mother makes a noise with the vacuum cleaner or shuts a door rather more loudly than usual.

"Ssssh!" she will say, frowning fiercely. "Can't you do that a little more quietly, please? You'll wake Muffin!

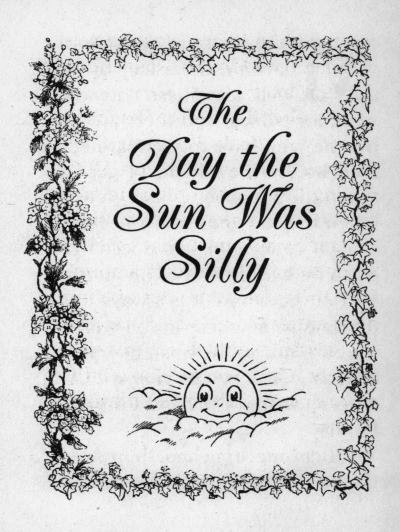

The Day the Sun Was Silly

MOST PEOPLE are awake in the daytime and asleep at night. Well, that doesn't always work for babies! And there are people who have to work at night as well. But on the whole, we get up when the sun gets up and go to bed when the sun goes to bed.

Of course, the sun doesn't really go to bed. It just shines on another part of the world. It is always daytime somewhere in the world. And it is always night somewhere else, as well. It works very well. We all get a share of the sun for part of the day.

But long, long ago, there was a day when the sun was very silly. All

day long, he had been shining down on a beautiful garden. There were flowers and trees, grass and fountains. It was lovely. The flowers lifted their pretty faces to say hello to the sun, and the tiny drops of water that jumped from the fountains sparkled like little jewels in the sunlight. The sun had never seen a more perfect sight.

"What a shame it will be night time soon," said the sun, "and I will not be able to shine on this garden any more. It's all very annoying. After all, I'm much bigger than anything else in the sky. I should be able to decide what I can do. No one's powerful enough to argue with me!"

So the silly sun carried on shining on the beautiful garden. The flowers stayed open, and the birds carried on singing.

But the garden wasn't meant to have sunshine all the time. Soon the flowers began to droop in the hot sun. The birds began to get hoarse from singing for so long.

The sun was stubborn. He wanted to prove that he could do anything he liked.

He was determined to carry on shining whatever happened.

Of course, the garden wasn't the only place that was in trouble. All over the world people were feeling very confused.

Streetlights came on and looked quite out of place in the bright sunshine. Animals that like to come out at night, such as owls, didn't know what to do. They were hungry, but it was much too bright to fly out of their nests.

In other parts of the world, there was the opposite problem. It was still dark, long after it should have been daytime. Some people were still in bed, asleep. Others tried to carry on as usual, eating their breakfast in the dark and setting off for work or school with torches. It was quite hopeless. And all because the silly sun thought he could do whatever he liked.

Meanwhile, the moon was getting very cross. If the sun kept shining, she couldn't be seen at all. The stars were invisible too.

Across the huge distances of space, the moon called out to the silly old sun.

"Hey! What do you think you're doing? Everything is dreadful on earth because you're not doing as you should. We all look up to you, you know."

When he heard that, the sun felt ashamed. He looked down on the beautiful garden and saw that the flowers were drooping and the birds were dropping off their perches with tiredness.

"They all rely on me," he thought. "I must be a sensible old sun in future."

And you know, from that day to this, he has never been silly again. Thank goodness!

Bubbles at Bathtime

ONCE UPON A TIME, there was a little boy who really hated his bathtime. He would yell and scream and kick his feet. It was terrible. And the funny thing is that there wasn't anything about his bath itself that he didn't like.

Here is what had happened. When Robert was a little tiny boy, he enjoyed being up and about so much that he never wanted to go to bed. He soon learned that bathtime meant bedtime would soon follow, so he started protesting as soon as his mummy began to run the water. It was dreadful. The yelling and screaming and kicking were so horrible that his poor mother dreaded bathtime more than cleaning the oven or opening the electricity bill.

The silly thing is that the yelling and screaming and kicking made Robert so tired that he always fell asleep the moment his mummy popped him into his little bed. So nobody realised that it was really bed-time and not bathtime he didn't like.

Sometimes we carry on doing things even when we can't remember why we do them any more. They become a habit. Bathtimes were like that for Robert. Although he was quite a big boy now, nearly old enough to go to school, he still made a dreadful fuss at bathtime.

One morning, Robert received a

surprise parcel. It wasn't his birthday or anything like that, so he couldn't wait to open it. Mummy looked at the writing and said she thought it was from Aunty Sue.

Robert liked Aunty Sue. She always sent him presents that were just right. He tore off the outer wrapping. Inside the brown paper was another parcel, wrapped in coloured paper. This one had a strange label:

My name is Bubbles

Whatever did *that* mean? As he ripped away the wrapping paper, Robert's face fell. Inside was a toy duck, the kind you have in the bath. It was quite a nice duck, certainly, with a yellow body and an orange beak, but still it was babyish, he thought. And anyway, it reminded him of that word beginning with *b*!

Robert pushed the duck across the table in disgust and hurried off to play.

That night, as Robert kicked and screamed in his bath, he noticed that his mother had put the duck on the shelf near the taps. Remembering his awful disappointment earlier in the day made Robert yell even more.

Just when Robert's poor mother was thinking that she couldn't stand *any* more, the telephone rang. There was a telephone out on the landing, so the poor woman quickly went to answer it, leaving the bathroom door open so that she could see her son all the time and make sure he was all right.

"Hello?" said Robert's mummy.

"Hello!" said Bubbles the duck. What? Robert stopped his

screaming for a moment in surprise. He thought for a moment that the duck had spoken, but of course that was silly.

"Hello," said Bubbles again. "It's Robert, isn't it?"

"Yes," said Robert, before he'd had time to think.

"Well, what's the trouble?" asked the duck in a friendly way.

"The trouble?" asked Robert, still not able to believe his ears.

"Yes. I couldn't help noticing, you see, that you were making quite a noise just now. Is something the matter?"

Robert shook his head like a puppy dog. He thought he might

have water in his ears. There must be some reason why he kept thinking the duck was speaking. And here it was doing it again!

"Well?" the duck persisted. "Is something wrong?"

"No," said Robert. "Yes, no!"

"You don't seem to be able to make up your mind," commented Bubbles. "Is the bath too hot or cold for you?"

"No," said Robert, rubbing his eyes in disbelief.

"Are you afraid of water?"

"No," said the little boy again.

"Well, is it soap you don't like?"

"No, soap is all right," said Robert, frowning.

"I'm sorry," said the duck. "I simply don't understand. Why were you screaming and yelling if you don't mind having a bath?"

Robert looked down. He felt rather silly.

"I don't know," he said.

"You don't know? A big boy like you? Well, that is very strange. I must say that in all my years of being in baths, I've never seen anything like it."

"Haven't you?" asked Robert, feeling very small.

"Certainly not," said the duck firmly. "Now is this kind of thing going to continue? Because I'm not sure I can live next to a bath that has such a noisy boy in it."

Robert thought for a minute. "I don't think I'm going to do it any more," he said, to his surprise.

"Good," said Bubbles. "Then I'll

be happy to stay and we'll be the best of friends."

Later that week, Robert heard his mother talking to a friend.

"You know," she said, "all these years of screaming and all he wanted was for me not to be in the room. After all, he's nearly old enough to go to school. Why ever didn't I think of it before?"

Well, I'm not going to tell her what really happened. Are you?